Balance IN CHAOS

BY
LILITH K. DUAT & MARIA DELYNN

BALANCE IN CHAOS

Printed in Canada
Print Edition - First Printing, 2015
ISBN 978-0-9939892-1-6

Broken Wings Media
brokenwingsmedia.com
Twitter.com/BWMSocial

Cover image by Caroline Guyer and used with permission.
http://www.teonova.com
Cover Illustration Copyright © 2014 by Broken Wings Media
Cover design by Lilith K. Duat.

BALANCE IN CHAOS

BY

Lilith K. Duat & Maria DeLynn

Balance in Chaos

ACT I

WAR.

It had to be war. The faces in the line, waiting to be judged, were unlike the faces of his people. The unfamiliar came in droves, waiting for his judgement.

Anup felt as if he had been weighing hearts of these dead invaders for centuries, but it had only been decades. Decades of the greatest slaughter to which he had ever bared witness. He was exhausted. It had to end.

He very rarely left his realm, his Underworld, yet now he allowed himself repose from the parade of souls, and rose up to the world of the living. All around him he saw the catastrophe. Ruined homes, strange, unnatural floods. Paths awash in blood.

War.

He could not abide this. He followed the trail of blood, which flowed from somewhere in the streets. As he tracked it, the streams of fluidic crimson grew and became thick. No longer were they small rivulets or meandering flows, but now well trodden paths and alleys between homes sank below the blood. And where there is blood, there is a heart.

Among ruined huts he saw her, standing atop a pile of corpses which were recently set aflame, the fire tracing a slow path from the ground up to where she posed. Her black wings playfully fed the fires and made them grow. She was laughing, a gilded, calm, aloof laugh.

"Discordia," he said with displeasure. "I might have known you were behind this chaos."

"What chaos is not my doing, hmm?" She turned her head, and her gaze slowly rose from the playful flames, her pale blue eyes now focusing on him. The wind picked up and made her white hair dance until threads tangled around the antlers on her head. The fire rode the wind from one hut to the next, leaping from roof to roof on the gusts. The flames lit the glistening red and brown path between them further and slowly started the destruction of the homes that surrounded them.

She laughed once again as a howling man came running out of a building with fire clinging to his back like a wet cloak. Screams came from the open door behind him. The man's family was trapped and all he was able do was thrash on the ground before the house, screaming along with them as his flesh cooked and sloughed from his muscles. He rolled and twisted his body in the mucky streets, putting out the flames as the roof of his house collapsed and the screams within were silenced. Unable to make a sound, he sobbed. The gods watched as the man began crawling, clawing his way slowly through the muck back to his silent household where he rested his head on the threshold.

Anup looked at the burning buildings, the screams and howls echoed from within the walls. He didn't seem to terribly disturbed other than mildly annoyed. He looked back at Discordia.

"I understand we cannot fight our nature. But we can practice restraint."

To that, Discordia rolled her eyes. "Restraint is no fun. This war is the only thing capable of entertaining me as of late. They're already being ripped apart by their own kind, I'm merely using their war as a canvas." She smirked, crossing her arms as she stared out past him at the bloody chaos.

"Yes, and you've made my existence hellaciously busy. I happened to be enjoying the quiet ages. The steady flow of births and deaths. The balance, the reliable constant. And yet, here you are, causing a backlog, clogging the arteries of my sacred halls. When Egypt dies, her people come to me. And I simply have no more patience for the strain."

She let out a short laugh. "Oh, you're very boring, shouldn't you be glad to be kept busy? The busier you are means the less bored you'll get." Discordia stretched then once again crossed her arms over her stomach. "I have no reason to stop, so go back to playing the good little god and return to your halls." Discordia turned her back to him. The long flowing skirt of her draping, sheer red dress swayed around her legs as she moved.

Anup narrowed his red eyes. "I need a rest." He said curtly, biting off each word.

"You've already rested enough for how long? Peace is boring, try to have some fun." She began walking, bent on raising more hell elsewhere. He followed her, stepping on the blackened corpses and through flames as if they were air.

"We are not finished with this discussion," he growled. He reached out to take her wrist and turn her to face him. "You're not used to being contradicted, are you?"

"And you're not used to actually having to deal with war. It will happen enough for you, you'll learn to like it." She tugged her hand out of his grasp.

"You believe that you are able to read me so easily," his muzzle was a mass of angry wrinkles and folded skin as he bared his teeth. "But you cannot even fathom. You would never be able to comprehend the absolute discipline my sacred role requires. You cannot even comprehend the very *notion* of discipline!"

Discordia smirked and flicked the angry god's nose. "Discipline is boring. I do not care to comprehend it nor will I ever try to. I like how things are for me, I am entertained. You are being nothing more than a downpour on my fun. The war will end in a few decades. Go back to where you came from."

Anup lunged for her and Discordia felt her back press against a ruined wall. She could feel the heat from the flames but her godly form was immune to being burned.

"Do not touch me." He snarled. "Do not ever touch me. You haven't the right or the grace to lay those calloused hands of yours on me."

"Someone's in a bad mood," her laugh was bold, and her face was inches from his snarling muzzle. "If you're so high and mighty, then why does a little clog in your stream of souls bother you so, hmm?"

Anup only continued to sound out a low growl of warning. His hands gripped harder on her shoulders, his claws pricking at her skin.

"You need to loosen up, Anup." She smirked at him. She tried to slip out of his grasp but the wall was a hindrance.

"Why would I take advice from an immoral girl such as yourself?" His voice shook with disapproval. Anup, and all the others gods of Egypt, had heard the legends of Zeus' unbound virility, of Zeus' many bastards, of the trickery he engaged in to create his offspring and make unwilling whores of Greek women. The unsavoury carnal appetites had tainted Olympus and dripped down to the bath houses where Greek boys serviced their men. It was no less surprising that Discordia knew only the same tactics.

"Morals are such a heavy burden to bear all the time, especially the number you seem to be saddled with. Slipping out from their yoke once in a while would be good for you, you might actually have some fun."

"This is not about you or I! These are my people you are toying with and you have no right to send them to the one that judges the souls of your kind. Even if you had such rights, I'd wager Hades would appreciate this flood of souls even less than I do. Go back to where you belong and play your games there, leave Egypt in peace."

She grinned impishly at him, "Mm, no? After all, I was banished. I'm free of rules and rulers now."

"You shallow, callous, careless, narcissistic shrew!" The red eyes of Anup stared into Discordia's own blue ones. His voice turned low, sullen and his gaze transformed from hateful, to full of pity. "To cause all this suffering on innocent lives... I cannot even begin to imagine how much hate and sorrow you must carry inside."

Her careless, laughing expression quickly reverted to anger. "I don't need your pity! And I have no sorrow." Her wings burst forth from her back as her struggle to be free of his grasp turned frantic.

"So she can be compelled." He sounded almost amused. "She can be bothered." The wings didn't seem to trouble Anup as they burst from her back and fanned the flames, causing them to swirl in small, scorching dervishes. "Why shouldn't I pity one who sees so little merit in the balance of nature?"

"Balance is nothing more than an Illusion you boring old fool!" She glared at him with narrowed eyes as she continued her struggle. "If you stopped trying to maintain the illusion and open your eyes, you might have some fun in your work."

"My job is far from 'fun'. My role is serious.

And *you* aren't leaving me time for fun even if I wished for any."

She blinked and her struggle slowed. Her blue eyes adopted a sparkle as an idea crossed her thoughts. Her expression softened and she smirked. "Well maybe I should give you a quick taste of fun," she purred, tilting her head up to him.

He hesitated, puzzlement clear on his face.

Discordia only snickered. "You poor thing, you don't even know what I'm talking about, do you? Well then..." She jerked her arm free of his hold and her hand went down, cupping his crotch.

Anup was startled by this bold action and recoiled slightly, his shoulders hunched and head looked down as his grip on her shoulders loosened. One hand hurried to the back of her neck, grasping it roughly, while the other shot down to enclose around her wrist. His grip was firm, threatening to break bones if he desired, but he left her hand against him, the grip only a warning.

"Calm down, it won't hurt. Now stop being so uptight." Her fingers moved and brushed against him through the skirt-like *shendyt* that hung from his hips. She ignored his grip, using her fingers to massage him softly. She smiled, pleased to learn that Anup seemed to be a man in all ways that mattered, except for his pitch black jackal head, of course. Under the fur, his body was warm as if he had been basking in the Egyptian sun. It was so unlike any other death god she had known. There was a sense of life to the warmth.

"Discordia…" Her name came out far more similar to a sigh than he had intended. "These things are not done…No good can come from this."

"Don't be such a bore. Have a little fun. You're a god, aren't you? What god hasn't had a little fun at least once?"

"I…" But any words of hesitance or rejection turned to ashes in the flames. His hand moved from the nape of her neck to the wall, his fingers pressing hard as if he were trying to keep himself centered.

"Just once. If you don't find it amusing, I'll leave Egypt and not cause any problems again." Her hand pressed harder against him as his grip became lax.

"I am not amused." He said bluntly. "Leave."

"You didn't even let me try," she pouted. "You need to let me really show you." Her eyes darkened. "Or I can continue sowing chaos with the same fervor as I'd have shown you." Her finger traced a long line as added emphasis.

"This is extortion," he growled. "You're keeping me hostage to your desires. It's no better than…" He trailed off and lowered his arrow-shaped head. If she made good on her threat, there was no way of knowing what hell she could rend or for how many decades she could keep it up before she became bored. He remained silent.

"Of course it is. Now then, I'm sure you will enjoy this more than you think." Her hands, after freeing her other arm from him, worked on undoing the fabric surrounding his lower body, exposing him. Her hand went back down to rub the still slightly limp length of him.

His hands were a blur as he took hold of her elk-like horns which formed a majestically twisted crown and added at least two feet to her height. He felt the bone and soft downy fur which covered them. He twisted her head to the right and pushed her down to her knees. "This is not our way. It is forbidden." He pushed her antlers back and it forced her head to tilt up. He glared down at her. "You are Olympian, your kind are here to overthrow mine!"

"Only the mortal men. I honestly couldn't care less over that. I'm only here for my own amusement." She forced her head forward against his grip, while she placed her hands demurely in her lap. She ran her tongue along the base of his fully aroused cock.

The hairs on the back of his shoulders and neck, down his spine, all raised up at the peculiar sensation along his most intimate parts. He gripped her horns tighter, fully aware he could use them to pull her away. Yet all he did was wring his hands along the branch-like growths and it caused his palms to burn. He exhaled through his nose, the skin under the erect fur twitching. He felt shame as parts of him reached for her, to be tasted by her tongue. Discordia took him deeper into her mouth and moved her head along his length. He wondered if she felt shame for this as well, or if she was only compelled to do such things for her own pleasure.

As her lips engulfed his length Anup opened his eyes to watch her. He was drawn in by the sight of her sunken cheeks, her sculpted nose, the perfect symmetry of her horns in his hands.

"By all that is, have some blasted dignity," he said with a harsh edge to his voice. But whether he was addressing Discordia or himself was unclear.

He felt her smirk and saw her eyes rise to meet his. She leaned her head away, making a soft popping noise when she pulled her mouth off his erection. Her tongue ran along the length as she stared up at him.

"Are you wanting me to stop already?" Her tongue circled the head softly, her blue eyes fixed to his as she waited for his answer.

He stood stiffly, not ready to give a response. She seemed well aware of his gaze as she continued to lick at him, like an animal washing her paw. His jaw tensed as his fists, still wrapped around her horns, moved her head so her mouth once again accepted him.

She chuckle softly before she opened her mouth and allowed him to slip in without complaint. She sucked him as her head moved along his length, the pace she moved was up to him, as he had the unrelenting grip on her antlers.

At first, it was slow, perhaps a bit boring to Discordia, but Anup was analysing it, studying it, quantifying it and trying to figure out what kind of pretty paper and bows to wrap it all up in to make it acceptable, even enjoyable. But there would be no re-packaging, no fables or fairy-tales.

She curled her tongue, teasing the base as she took the head and more down her throat. She swallowed him down and caused a strange but alluring pull against his member. It caused him to let out a broken moan.

She once again smirked. This was the sound she had been looking for from him. He was enjoying himself, loosening up just a little. Her tongue rubbed against his length as she sucked on him. A hand went up to cup his sack, her fingers massaging it lightly as her mouth worked on him. His eyes closed, and he was lost in sensation and pleasure. He opened his eyes and looked down and once again saw the filthy beauty of her perfect symmetry. The bones caused flawless shapes under her skin and the shadows created and accentuated contours and colours. His fuzzed mind told him she seemed to be glowing.

His hips moved and he pushed himself deep down her throat.

She let out a moan at that, the sound causing her tongue to vibrate slightly against his length. With a gentle hand she continued to knead his sack, the other hand cupped one of his ass cheeks, the fingers lightly stroked through his soft fur.

He grunted, back twitching as her fingers weaved through his fur. His back arched, a buzz rolling up his spine. Her nose buried into the fur on his belly as she took his length as far as possible. Sounds of a panicked pleasure filled Discordia's ears as she swallowed against him, humming playfully.

The sounds were like sweet music to her. She wondered how long it would take for this to get far more fun, but she had to bide her time. After all, he was so high-strung. But that did not mean she could not encourage the process.

She leaned her head back and pulled him from her throat, then her tongue flashed across the shining head of his cock rapidly, fluttering against it like the wings of a hummingbird, grazing it with butterfly touches and serpent allure. Her tongue slashed back and forth from her lips, snapping and tickling at the very end of his nerves. Her hand abandoned his back and enclosed around the base of his shaft. She began to pump, guiding his hips to a rhythm. His muscles drew tight and she closed her lips around him.

Anup gasped and Discordia savoured him as he coated her tongue. He breathed heavily, stewing in the rapture. It was a rejuvenation he had not experienced in so long that it slipped from his memories, if he ever had them to begin with. He opened his eyes and looked down at her. His hands were still on her antlers. He pulled her to her feet and yelled "Away!"

He pushed her back, into the wall. Her tongue, splitting through her cruel grin, dripped of him.

She laughed, taking a moment to swallow the glistening stuff. "I had thought you would have stopped earlier if you had not enjoyed it. Or do you not have as much discipline as you claim?" Her tongue ran along her lips.

He stood before her, still bared to her, guilt and shame and above all, a fire of lust in his eyes.

"Away!" He said again as he gripped her shoulders and turned her to face the scorched and ruined wall. Her ass brushed against his exposed organ not entirely on accident. Discordia tried to look at him over her shoulder but was met by jaws clamping down on her right antler.

Discordia gasped, her fists clenched where her hands rested on the ruined wall. She honestly had not expected such a thing. Not wanting to lose control of the opportunity he presented, she moved her ass against him.

Another growl, one of anger and craving. His slick, wet cock slid across the hills of her ass and left a thin trail of his seed diluted by her saliva. It made the red fabric of her dress stick to her pale skin. He moved his hips back, trying to put distance between their bodies.

She moved her hips, keeping her ass pressed against his erection. Her dress slipped from her shoulders, dangerously close to exposing her entire chest. "Why deny what you want, hmm?"

Another frustrated growl and he pulled away

fully. His sharp teeth left grooves in her antlers as he unlocked his jaws. He took a step back and watched as she turned around. Then, he began to laugh deeply.

"Don't you see? You degraded yourself for my pleasure. I could walk away right now, knowing I had you exactly as I wanted you. You think yourself to be the one in control, the one with all the power. But you gladly took my offering while perched upon soot-sodden knees on scorched earth. I got what I wanted. I calmed your fires and received my own pleasure. We're done here."

"Oh, you haven't even *begun* to calm my fires." The air itself seemed to scream as her eyes flashed. "I believe another several thousand souls have just entered your domain." She smirked. "If I don't get my satisfaction, your job will grow, just as my newly ignited fires have." Then she turned, not even bothering to cover herself or straighten her dress as she walked away from him. She had nothing more to say.

His shoulders sank in exasperation and his head dropped limply. He could hear her walking away as his downward gaze caught his softening cock. "Why do you do these things? Is it because you are your brother's sister? Are you compelled to follow your brother's lead? You are aware you are a separate entity than him."

"That is none of your business." She snapped at him, stopping and turning towards him. "And I am more than aware that I am separate from Ares!"

He raised his head. "Are you?" he asked. "Then how do you see yourself?"

"Once again, it is not your concern." An angry sneer molded itself to her face. The truth of it was that she simply did not know. She realized that, much like a spoiled child, she simply did what she wanted.

He stepped through the flames, ash particles swirling up his feet and making abstract patterns in the air. "When I look upon you, I see a being which has the potential to be one of nature's greatest mothers. Your antlers, far reaching like the roots weaving through the earth." He cupped her cheeks. "The blue of all the oceans and seas and rains in your pale eyes." His hands trailed down, his thumbs going over the sculpt of her throat, his palms over her shoulder, "The winds in your breath, your voice. Your wings." His hands went lower still, palms slipping down over her collarbone, over her full, partially exposed breasts. "And the fire..." His hands went down more, past her ribs, her stomach, to rest over her womb. "In your loins. You could perpetuate life, Discordia. Not squander it. Not defile it."

She paused, her eyes widened slightly. She had never been told such sweet things before. Was she too stuck in her ways? For a moment, she seemed consider his words. She cast aside the thoughts and let the power of his words fall from her mind. It would take far more than mere words to tame her, calm her enough to obtain her true potential. Her eyes narrowed and she smacked his hands away.

"None of what you say is true. Your sweetened words won't stop me. I am how I am now, and always will be."

"Look around you," his hands slid up to her shoulders. "Change is all around us. Egypt is spoiled with change. Now is the perfect time to become someone new."

Her momentary rage faltered. Her gaze went downwards to the ashen and dirty ground. Flames appeared and licked them, the fire spreading around the village. "I...don't know how to change."

He took a chance and reached his hand out, nudging her chin up and directing her gaze to his face.

"As a goddess of chaos you must know that chaos is change. This street will never be as it was after this fire. And blistering heat from fire is what some seeds of great trees need to blossom. Perhaps this street will be a garden in the future. Perhaps these flames will spark you to grow too."

"How?" Her voice was sharp, yet despite her frustration, she didn't push him away. "How does one truly change when they've already settled into one way of life?"

"I don't know," he confessed. "Yet I have faith. Belief. We are beings made of pure faith and belief. Perhaps the belief of one is all that it takes."

"If we are made of faith and belief, who out

there will believe that I can change when I've been this way for so long? I can barely believe that I'll change. I've already been labeled a cruel goddess."

"Perhaps the belief of a god is more powerful than that of even ten-billion humans. And I believe."

She blinked, her mouth slightly a gap in shock. "You do?"

"If I didn't, I would have said nothing about it. But I did. Because I do."

"Why?" She asked. She was rather confused.

"Don't question it," he shook his head. "But I know you are more than capable of proving me right." He dared to cup her head in his hands. "And you'd be far more satisfied, something greater, more loved and worshipped."

Once again, she frowned. She allowed him to cup her face but her eyes were cast downwards. "No one has ever told me that I could be something different, something better than what I am now. I don't know...I suppose I can try change. Throw some chaos into myself. It might even be fun." She smiled. "Since you're determined to not let me have my normal fun here."

He nodded, then pressed a blessed kiss on her forehead, between the root of her antlers. "Go forth. And try." He released her cheeks and ran his hands down her wings. From one wing, he plucked a loose black feather. "A souvenir. I may not fully approve of what happened, but that doesn't mean I wish to forget it completely."

She opened her mouth with a smirk as if to leave a biting remark but reconsidered, smiling to herself, holding her thoughts private. She nodded after a moment. "...Thank you." Then with a flash she was gone.

He looked around at the fires and the ash, the ruined buildings and the streets of blood. He sighed, hoping that the war would soon end and the disasters she brought forth would fade. He brought the feather to his nose and inhaled, catching the faint scent of her. While his workload would return to its normalcy, he wondered how far she would run from hers.

Anup returned to Duat, his Land of the Dead, with a long exhale and a crack of his neck. There was a silent, unmoving parade of lost souls, their faces showing fright and confusion, all waiting to be judged. Anup passed through the line, shouldering lost souls out of the way and walking to his scales. He rolled Discordia's feather in his fingers and it fluttered into tight, tiny circles among his claws.

He conjured the Feather of Truth, then a moment of curiosity captured the deity as he looked upon his perfectly balanced scales. He placed the Feather of Truth in the left-most scale pan as if in preparation to weigh the hearts of the recently deceased but instead he placed Discordia's endlessly black feather in the other pan of the scales. The equilibrium was instantly eradicated as Discordia's feather could not disguise how heavy with sorrow and horror it was. Anup hung his head, sadly ruminating to himself that if her single feather was so burdened with guilt and venom, he could not imagine how heavy her heart must have been. It put the shadows of doubt on his own heart.

He plucked the black feather from the scales and tucked it away in his belt, then turned his attention to the long line of those waiting to be judged.

Discordia sat upon a cliff above a river and poked at spiderwebs with blades of grass. The water rushed and tumbled far below her, the pounding roar echoing up from the valley and filling her ears, the fresh scent strong. She looked down upon the water below with a sigh. She was far from anything now, the chaos she had brought had ended. She was unsure what to do with herself, and the more she thought about wanting to change…

How was it Anup believed in her? He didn't truly know her after all. He just wanted her to end the chaos she had reigned down upon his home.

Despite that, his words stuck with her, worming their way into her mind. What if she did turn her affinity for chaos inward, inspiring change of her own being? Maybe she could become a good god, one which mortals were happy to worship, one who was unfeared by humans. Yet questions remained; where would she start? How would she start? She sighed and looked up to the sky. She had no clue, but the seed of motivation was there. She just needed a little more of a nudge to make the change happen. A little more fire.

As she contemplated, sweet coincidence loomed. While the river bubbled and babbled, the clear water began to grow red like wine, then redder still, like blood. Butchered, bloated bodies floated along the currents without complaint. Their faces were frozen in horror and pain. Walking, marching, knee deep in the pink foam settled on the surface of the river of agony came Ares.

"Hello, brother." Discordia spoke normally, knowing her voice would carry clearly through the distance to his ears. She looked down at him. With him around, keeping her word would become rather...difficult. After all, she had always followed her brother's plans, which lead to her causing horrific chaos. Despite her wish to change, she still looked up to him.

"You know, Discordia." He started, smoothly. He reached up and pulled the ram-horn helmet from his head with force enough to rip a human's skull free from its shoulders. "I was over in Rhakotis, with the great king Alexander, helping him cut down the Egyptian nothings who were making inconveniences of themselves, and do you know what I realized?"

"What did you realize?" Discordia asked, not

moving from her seat on the ground. She eyed him, unsure of where he was going with this.

"I realized," he stepped from the water and began walking on the floating corpses as if they were solid ground. When he reached the cliff wall on which Discordia was perched, he planted a foot, wet with blood, onto it and effortlessly walked up it, giving not a care to gravity or natural law. Fully horizontal he walked up the cliff as if it were flat ground, back faced the river, his face focused to hers. "That the people of Rhakotis were putting up an exceptionally well organized and tenacious resistance."

He was a mere few meters from the shelf of the cliff upon which Discordia sat, yet he never reached it. Instead, he was gone from her vision.

A hand closed around Discordia's throat, tight, crushing. "I realized that there was no surprise, no confusion. There was no...chaos."

She grabbed his hand and tried to pry it off. "I got bored with them," she gasped out. Telling him how Anup had put new possibilities in her mind would not be a wise move, so she decided that boredom, as with anything else, would be her reasoning for doing or not doing something.

"I do not care what you thought of them," he sneered calmly into her ear. "I gave you a task. I expect you to see it through until the end."

His fist came down hard on the back of her skull, then he let her go. He watched as she tumbled backward into the dirt. He grabbed her by an antler and dragged her back around towards the precipice. Dirt and sand scratched along her cheeks and eyes. He threw her forward as if cracking a whip and she landed with a thud, sliding over the dirt and rocks until she nearly went over the edge. She stopped with her shoulders over the edge, her legs splayed on the ground to keep her from sliding fully off into the floating graveyard below. Ares foot pressed firmly on her upper back between her wings, and he leaned down to seize her horns.

"Look," he yelled, pointing her face to the river below, choked with bodies. "Look at this pitiful tally. And look how many are our people!"

She clenched her jaw. "When was the last time I cared? I only care if it entertains me. After all, I learned that from you, dearest brother," she sneered as she spoke. "You cannot make me do anything I do not wish to do."

Ares wrenched her back by the horns while his foot kept her hips and legs planted firmly on the dirt. Discordia felt a pop in her shoulder blade. Ares stumbled off her and threw her again, away from the cliff. She tumbled through the dirt, shoulder over wing, arm over rib.

He grabbed her by the horns once more, only to throw her away again. On and on it went, seemingly forever. He tossed her around as if she were a sack of soiled sheets, a bale of hay for his war horses, the enemy's flag to disgrace.

He grabbed her again, one hand on each horn and he dragged her to her knees. He stared with angry hatred into her pitch-black eyes. He pulled, as if dividing a woman's legs. She could feel her skull begin to split apart at the crown, between the eyes, and down her nose. With the most incredible pop of pain, Discordia felt a terrifying lightness and she fell from her brother's hold.

She hit the ground with a agonized cry. Her hands hurried to the top of her head, then ran through her long white hair. Her horns had always been there and now they simply were not. It hurt. She had never before felt pain like this.

Her dark eyes narrowed, glaring up at him. "I will not change my mind," she growled at him, her voice thick with agony.

He gathered her two horns into one fist and they clattered together like sticks. His armored sandal met with her cheek and she fell to her side. He kicked her onto her belly.

Discordia felt his foot on her spine once more. He grabbed her wings in each fist and pulled. Her figure arched back like Artemis' crescent hunting bow, her eyes shut as she cried out, and with a wet tearing sound, her wings were ripped free from her body.

She fell forward.

When Discordia awoke, she was on her back. She

saw her wings, one on either side of her, full and extended as if in flight. Each wing was pierced just below the elbow joint by one of her sharp, severed antlers.

She let out a sob, the pain was unbearable. Blood dripped down her face from the tear in her skull, her skin split. She looked hideous now. She sat up, every movement brought searing pain through her body. She grabbed her antlers and tried to pull them out. The open wounds on her back screamed and strangled the muscles needed to free her wings in red hot pain; rendering the effort she needed to exert in order to free them was impossible. She pulled and yanked for hours, and bit by bit, she managed to free the wings from the horns. After the ordeal of freeing the wings she rested for another hour before forcing herself to her feet. She gathered her antlers in one hand then picked up the wings and bundled them under her arm. What was she going to do now?

She limped her way towards the place she had met Anup. She had nowhere else to go.

By the time she had arrived at the small, ruined village, Discordia was all but crawling through the hot ash and charred bones which remained. Her surroundings reeked. The embers, floating like fireflies, caught in her wounds and burned her. She sought shelter, and shuffled through the doorway of one of the ruined huts.

Yet, when she passed through the door, she was not inside the hut, but rather in a large chamber.

It was dark and cool, but comfortable. Pillars were decorated with images which formed words, words which formed stories. Wall sconces cradled lit torches and illuminated the place. The stone tiled floor was dusted with cool sand which rested in gentle dunes along corners and edges of the walls. There was no celing, only darkness.

It was nice, the chill cooled and soothed her body, which burned with rage and the fiery pain of shorn flesh. She closed her eyes, not really caring where she was. She couldn't move anymore anyway. She was too weak.

Discordia was distantly aware of strong arms lifting her and carrying her away. Was she being taken to oblivion? Being born anew? Being reborn mortal? She could not think of a worse fate but couldn't raise the energy to put up a true fight. She struggled against the being who held her, but she was weak and no better than a mewling kitten.

"I will not harm you," Anup told her quietly. She recognized his voice and became still in his cradling hold.

Anup placed Discordia on a surface, laying the wings at either side and her horns just above her head. His claws moved along her figure. Stoically, yet carefully, he removed the swaths of red fabric which were once her tattered and torn gown until she was nude. With a great deal of gentleness, he began to wash her body in a cleansing liquid of sweet-smelling palm wine.

The cold, dried blood was wiped away from her now hideous face. "Why?" Was the only word she could utter.

His scented hand went to her brow and he stroked the fissure in her forehead with his thumb. The gesture was strangely serene. He said nothing.

His cleansing hands slipped along every part of her wounded form, purifying her as best as her evil vessel could be purified. He moved to one end of the surface and lifted her head, fanning her hair out like a peacock's plume. He stroked her scalp before covering her eyes with a hand. He poured the cool, fragrant wine through her hair, letting it rinse away the blood.

The sensation caused a sigh to escape her lips. The cleansing wine cooled the hot, searing pain of her head. She closed her eyes beneath his hand, gave in and relaxed. His hands once again massaged her body. He pushed her feet to point, so the bath would roll off her toes. He lightly lifted her breasts to wash away the mud and ash from underneath. He probed a finger under her knee, causing her leg to bend. The scented liquid cascaded down her thigh and puddled between her legs, then drained down into a jar.

He tended to her wings next, basting them in fresh palm wine. The wine beaded on the wings as does oil on water. It slid through the forest of slick, black feathers, shimmering like liquid gold in the torchlight as the wine forced blood to join it in the jar.

The antlers were washed as well, though there was little to be done with them. They were hard, unyielding things. They seemed to defy the wine bath.

He passed water over Discordia, rinsing away the lingering blood and horror. He stroked her flesh, pushing the water down, and along her body, banishing it from pooling on her belly or throat or her wounds.

She opened her eyes, the color once again a pale blue. She was serene, relaxed as she watched him.

"Thank you," she said softly.

He offered a hand to help her sit up, then poured the water down, from one shoulder, past her neck, to the other, rinsing away the blood from her back. He ran a wet, sweet-smelling cloth down her spine with a hand, dragging his other hand down her front, slowly, checking for lingering filth.

She placed her hand over his when it went to her stomach and guided it down to between her thighs. She said nothing but he knew what she wanted. Her intentions were clear.

Anup thought little of Discordia's guidance until he felt the folds of her with his fingertips. He looked at her but said nothing. Nor did he put up a resistance as she continued to guide his touch. He cupped her in the palm of his hand. He rubbed, light, slow. He knew Discordia's intentions were far from pure, but if a little bit of carnal excitement placated her pain, then a healing touch was necessary.

She held herself and rocked, rather like a child. She was just trying to soothe herself, to banish the agony. Her eyes closed, the pleasure mixed with the pain. Soon enough his fingers made the pain fade to the back of her mind.

He stroked her, massaged her, touched her softly. He tricked little moans into escaping her throat. Then, without a word, he drew back and his hands left her body.

"Who did this?" There was no rage or fear or glee in his voice, just a hint of empathy. He pushed her long hair over her shoulder. It was still wet and smelling of palm-wine. He began to wind a linen wrap around her chest, securing the wings once again to their proper place at her back. It would take time to heal. He placed many wraps around her, occasionally placing amulets of protection between the layers, murmuring incantations as he worked.

"My brother. Ares." She said. Her eyes followed his hands as he wrapped the white linen strips around her. It was mesmerizing in a way. "I refused to go back on my word to you and he retaliated."

"Then...in a way...I did this to you."

"No. I didn't even tell him, I gave my word. I just told him I was bored. This is just what happens if I don't listen to my brother. Even chaos must abide by some sort of rule." She sighed.

"There is little I can do for your skull other

than give it time and keep it clean." He said. He produced a string with small amulets dangling from it. He placed it over her head like a crown. "There is even less I can do for your horns. I'm sorry. Perhaps Sekhmet will have better remedies. Something of more potency."

"It's alright. I can live without my horns as long as I have my wings." Her pain was a dull throb now. "What are those for?" She asked, lightly touching one of amulets which dangled from the delicate chain.

"Healing," he replied. "And protection." He stepped back from the slab she sat on and reached out his hand. "Follow me. I will take you somewhere you can rest."

They walked through the halls of the Necropolis side by side as he guided her. It was cool, and quiet. He brought her to a room where a bed was draped in sheer curtains. "It is not much, but you're safe here. Try to rest."

Discordia was unable to sleep, not after all that had happened. His fingers had left her wanting and the ache was returning to her body. She needed him. She sat up from the comfortable bed on which he had left her and she made her way to where he slept.

Anup's bed was a simple, slightly bowed table with a headboard. It was covered in cushions and the sheet draping over his body was linen. Laying on the bed, he resembled a pharaoh's sarcophagus carved from wood and stone by the hand of a master. Only the rise and fall of his chest hinted of his godly flesh.

She climbed on top and straddled his hips as her fingers ran through the soft fur along his chest and stomach. Anup stirred but he did not wake. His hips shifted under her and Discordia felt her body gently rise then fall, like she was riding a horse at a light gait.

She slid the linen sheets down, her lips pressed against his neck as her hands roamed his body once the sheet was out of the way.

While it was cooler than Egypt above in here, the flames in the sconces throughout his bedchamber burned hot. Beneath the sheets, he was nude. Discordia was greeted by a slightly aroused organ of hardening flesh. Her hand wrapped around the length and she began to massage it. Her arousal heightened the sensations across her skin. She was nude save for the rough bandages Anup had wound around her body, but those merely covered her injuries and the clean slick fur tickled her thighs.

He enthusiastically grew in her hold, and muttered out a sleepy sound. His head turned from one cheek to the other. He lifted his hand and reached out. Was he about to touch her?

He grabbed the sheet and pulled it up again, but now it was over Discordia as well. The linen was so very soft.

She smirked slightly, sliding down beneath the sheets. Her lips pressed against the tip of him before running her tongue along his shaft. His organ reacted pleasingly to her tongue and it grew straight and amorous. His was a rather handsome and proud looking cock.

Anup opened his eyes and pulled back the sheet. He looked down the length of his body and saw Discordia's mischievous blue eyes giving him a mirthful glance as he watched her trace the outline of his hard member with her wet, blood-red tongue.

She took the tip into her mouth and sucked sharply on it. She slid down so his cock was fully inside of her mouth with a soft moan. The feeling of him on her tongue was blissful. Of course it would have been a better sight for him if her skull was still together, but the bandages he had placed on her hid most of it. Any mortal would have feared the hideous sight she had become, but Anup was no mortal.

This time, he did not question it. This time, he did not fight it. He thought her too much a wounded creature to make her suffer any more pain or rejection. He sat up and sucked in a breath as his cock was caressed by the walls of her throat. He brushed back her white hair, he missed the symmetry of her horns, their arrogant beauty. His palms itched. His knuckles felt of stone. He wanted so much to grab her horns and hold them one more time.

He reached down and put a hand on her

head, between the gravestone crown of her broken horns. He eased her away from his cock and watched as she slowly moved to straddle his lap. Her sex cradled his length as she moved her hips to rub her fresh dampness against his hard shaft. Her tongue ran along his snout and he nuzzled it. She moved her hand between them, a guide for him as her hips moved to take him inside. She moaned as she felt him slide slowly within her, her muscles contracting against him to indulge in every impure delight she could lure from his flesh into hers.

He was all she needed in this moment, filling her completely with pleasure and heat and a soothing pressure. It gave her a feeling of...not being empty. For how long had she felt empty? But his presence, the intoxication he provided, was a comfort.

As he sat up and wrapped his strong arms around her, it made her feel defended, protected. As he held her close, and claimed her body for his own uses, she felt delight and thrill, a thrill which slaughter and chaos did not bring her. The brasiers full of tongues of fire cast their entwined shadows on the walls and made them dance as he bucked his powerful hips up in between her thighs.

Discordia let out soft noises filled with rapture. She felt warm, whole, safe. Something scarce for her. Of course she knew such things would not last, but she would take it for as long as she possibly could, savoring the feeling of him inside of her.

Anup held her almost as one would a small

scared child seeking comfort, but he moved within her like some sort of demon possessed and the strange juxtaposition of both of these traits drove Discordia wild inside. Her loins burned while her heart fluttered and she dragged her nails to cut against his strong back. She let out carnal cries, her eyes unfocused as she gazed over Anup's shoulder, watching the shadows flicker. It looked almost like the shadows were coming closer, but her mind was too hazy with euphoria to truly take note.

His slick fur was like soft, short, freshly cut grass against her hands as she rode him. He gripped her hair with both his hands and pulled her head back as he licked her throat. Their shadows were on the ceiling, behaving in ways just as obscene and delicate as Anup and she. As he snarled and spilled his fountain of ecstasy deep inside her, the shadows seemed to gather and coalesce, expanding from the surface of the cavern down towards the entangled gods. The falling shadow passed through them both, tinging the joyful blush they both felt with a cold, burning chill. As she arched her back in climax, wings of shadow fanned out wide, and seemed to peel from the stones as the figure rose and gathered itself. The darkness flashed once more over their bodies in a swirl of fabric and midnight, before vanishing, leaving only the flickering dance of the flame on the ceiling above them as evidence of the passing.

Discordia collapsed onto Anup, her head

laying now on his chest. She panted as she caught her breath. She watched the shadows play on the stone walls. The shadows coalesced into the form that had appeared over them, winged and tall, the shape solidifying as it wandered about the room as a cloaked figure of a man too tall to be human, wings spread wide from his back. It lingered as it walked in the dark corners of the room. She watched it with interest as she lay upon Anup. She silently counted each feather on each extended wing, like a new parent with the fingers of their first born. This deathly shadow, with a thousand feathers on each wing, seemed to be a sign of their union.

On Earth above them, war continued to rage. Wherever Ares stepped, men slaughtered one another. The trail he left was scarred and bloody. He would have been angry with his sister's disobedience, but it was the nature of chaos to not follow rules. In the grand scheme, it didn't matter; Ares enjoyed his work.

In the fires made by war came a shadow. Where it roamed, there was the metallic din of a sistrum. It smelled of sweet-wine and apples. It floated along the beaten path laid by Ares, gliding just above the mangled corpses and strewn gore. And all it could hear were screams.

Souls trapped just under the flesh and bone of the dead thrashed against the skin and sinew, begging for release. The shadow spread its black wings of smoke and scorched dreams. He lifted his stave of Egyptian gold and Greek silver and slid the sickle blade down into the corpse, cutting the ethereal barrier which kept the soul bound to the bag of bones. The soul was then embraced by the wings and enfolded among the burnt linen, clattering bronze plates and patchwork leather of the shadow's robes.

Once it was known that one soul could be untethered, the others clamored, clawing at the cold, clammy skin of their bodies. They cried out, yearning to be unbound from this prison. Grimly, they were freed one-by-one.

The shadow released dozens, then hundreds, then hundreds of thousands. He embraced them all into the folds of his black cloak. There they stayed, protected by the midnight of his robes and the shelter of his ribcage. They slept in limbo until such a time they would settle on their final resting place.

<><><>

"Is it true?" Anup asked. He lay with Discordia on his bed, and together they were enjoying a carafe of wine and a platter of assorted fruits and meats. "In the village you had said that you were exiled. For what reason? And why did they not strip you of your power? Why had you not been made mortal?"

Discordia looked at the platter and plucked up a slice of apple. "Apples."

Anup looked skeptical. "Apples?"

"Just one. One little apple." She bit the crisp apple wedge in half. "A gift for the fairest goddess of them all. Trouble was they couldn't agree on who indeed was the fairest. They asked an impartial mortal to judge and those who claimed the title tempted him. The situation escalated until it triggered a war that waged across seas." She sighed, "the war was unexpected, and delighted Ares. In thanks, my brother made sure that I was not made mortal, he wanted me to continue with my work. He enjoyed the show even more than I," Discordia sipped the sweet wine.

"I see," Anup replied. "And in exchange for the favour he did for you, you are required to…" He took a guess. "Aid him in his battles? Make them as vile and as full of butchery as possible?"

"He told me to just do as he said, so yes, part of it was to aid in battle." She licked her lips. "Favours often come at a cost, and war is often brought on by broken treaties. Even chaos has rules to abide."

Anup looked down into his goblet. "…had I known…"

She looked at him. "What would you have done, had you known? My brother is stronger than I. My fate there would not have changed."

"Had I not interfered, you would have remained loyal. You would have not been punished for…thinking for yourself." He tossed back his head and took a long drink of his wine. "I inspired those thoughts in your mind. And I am no muse."

"And had you not interfered then you would be getting more souls coming to you for judgement." She ran her fingers through the silky fur on his head. "But I thank you for coming to my aid after all that was done. You kept me from my brother, were he to return and make me endure more of his wrath."

He closed his eyes, killing the red glow they emitted and bathing his face in the shadows. As he felt her touch, he privately marveled at how fingers which had sewn so much catastrophe and dour histories could possibly be so light and tender.

Her fingers massaged his scalp before sliding her hand down to his chest, then further down. Discordia seemed incapable of innocent touches for long.

He grabbed her wrist and his eyes opened. They gazed at her, a smouldering crimson. "I did not bring you here with the intent of using you for my own pleasure," he told her. "Your submission is not necessary."

"Who said I was submitting to you?" Her fingers brushed against him, "I get pleasure from doing such things."

Anup put forth no more resistance. Instead he reached for the platter of fruit and plucked up a fat, red cherry. He dropped it in his mouth and reached for another one. He held it carefully by the thin stem and offered it to Discordia. Her lips brushed his fingers as she took the stem partially into her mouth. She popped the cherry off the stem and pulled her mouth away.

He put his hand on the small of her back and ran his tongue from her shoulder to her jaw. He exhaled against her skin and felt her hand explore. Her hand rubbed when she found his length and she kissed the side of his muzzle.

"You should be resting," he muttered, offering her a slice of apple. She took it in her mouth, sucking on his fingers which slid softly along her plush lips. He caressed her jaw, her neck. His hips jumped forward in response to her grip. "Healing."

"I can heal well enough like this." Her lips pressed against the palm of his hand. Her nimble fingers massaged his length. He slipped another grape past her lips and it rolled onto her tongue. He kissed her as her teeth came down. The fruit exploded against her cheeks in a burst of juice like a cold arterial spray. She shared the sweet, tart taste of the grape with him as his sharp fangs grazed and tugged at her lips.

She let out a soft sound as the taste of the grape mingled on their tongues. The sharp prick of his edged fangs on her lips just made snaps and bolts of delight course through her.

The hand which rested on the small of her back deftly slid around her and he held her. He kept weight off her healing wings as in one move he pulled her to his lap and lay her down on his bed. He loomed over her, dark and powerful. His gaze studied her face, her body. Once more. One last time. Then never again. No one knew the truth of how Anup and Discordia were spending their time, or even that they had even known one another and so there was no consequence, nothing lost nor gained. For now there was the freedom and secrecy of this moment.

Discordia did wish for this to never end, but they both knew their fun couldn't continue much longer. Her hands glided over his strong body, memorizing the shape and contours of his form. She moaned, the sensation of his silky fur sent a tingle through her limbs and up her back. Her legs went around his hips, bringing him closer and sending a wave of warmth through her. The doubts about her wings ever becoming part of her again were dashed as they shuddered against the bondage of the healing wraps. They hurt, but they were once again a part of her.

He growled softly as her hands traced his hard stomach, reaching between them. He felt her thighs tighten around him. When her wings trembled against his arm he was stunned. She was healing.

She let out a soft cry as he moved within her. The bandages fell away as her wings splayed out behind her, once more the proud, graceful wings they had always been. The bandages began slipping down from her torso as she swayed and danced under him, the bruises and cuts a seemingly distant memory.

As he saw the bandages begin to unravel he put an arm under her and rolled onto his back, their bodies still locked, hips rocking, with her now on top. He watched in awe as the linens unfurled from her feathers and fluttered down, hanging loosely on the proud black wings like crepe paper from a forgotten party. The air peeled through his fur as her wings gave a flap, discarding the bandages. She rode him. With each bounce and shift the wraps around her body loosened. Her pale white skin shone beneath the sun-bleached beige wrappings, rather than angry pink and red scars.

Soon the bandages around her skull fell, her skin that beautiful pale white, her white hair cascaded freely behind her and dropped over part of her wings. Little nubs of horn poked through the strands of her hair, coming out of where her old horns had once been.

This part of his underworld was dark and she seemed to glow a spectral silver. The pureness of her white flesh and hair was incongruent with her nature. The conflict between appearance and reality made her unique and a mystery to Anup. He reached up and started to pull the lifeless wrappings from her body. They were thin and soft and pliant. They whispered as they slid from her skin. He dropped them onto the floor absently.

Her body moved, oblivious to the bandages he peeled from her skin. The elation she felt seemed to almost blind her to anything other than Anup and herself. She leaned down and her hand went to the back of his head, once again petting him, her fingers massaging his head as her body moved.

He watched her. Her white skin and the awesome span of her freshly woven wings brought to mind images of celestial beings which Anup had no words for. The only way he could describe it was to say she was 'divine', but he dismissed it for being too weak a word. She seemed the most beautiful and sacred creature he had even beheld, and he could easily understand mortals laying prostrate in worship of her. Something meant for the heavens, fallen down to his depths. He briefly forgot about Discordia's true nature.

Whenever she was with him, her malicious chaos seem to vanish, even if only for a short period of time. For now she was in bliss, her body humming.

He moaned and arched his back. He threw himself to sit up and he embraced her under her wings. He licked and sucked her now perfect breasts, leaving fresh bruises and pink welts where he bit. Discordia's back arched as his teeth teased her nipples. Her hands cradled his head as she shifted her weight backwards, slamming down onto her back. Her wings were still fanned out, her hair tangled among the feathers.

His hands traveled up along her sides, feeling the dips and hills of her ribs as she writhed like grass in a storm under him. He squeezed her breasts and gathered all of her flaws into his hand. She continuously cried out. Her wings flapped, the cool air going through his fur. Anup sat up on his knees and grabbed her wrists from his head. Her fingers raked through his black fur and mussed it about. He leaned forward, pinning her arms above her fanned out wings. He leaned back down and thrust deep inside of her with renewed craving as his ecstasy quickly climbed toward its zenith.

His pent up lust could no longer remain contained and all that energy released from his form out into the universe. Above them, and below the feet of the human warriors, the earth shook with the power of their joined passion.

Her hips rocked against his, pleasure shooting up through her, triggered by his hurried thrusts, spreading to the tips of her wings. She let out a fresh chorus of cries which harmonized with his.

Discordia's realm was primordial, one she had to keep tethered tightly. Her's was a controlled chaos and should she slip, natural laws were forfeit. As she was lost in complete ecstasy, her voice caused thunder and lightning within the human realm. Her worshippers and god-fearers felt unimaginable pleasure before their bodies burst into flame, or they slit their own stomachs with sacrificial knives.

He wrapped an arm under the small of her back and took her hand with his other as he sat back so she straddled his lap. He was panting, and he watched her wings as they calmed their hurricane force flapping. They stared at each other for what felt like hours, and their natural disasters calmed in the human world.

"You are once more whole." Anup ran his hand along her inner wing.

"I would not have been, had it not been thanks to you." She leaned her forehead against his. Her horns once again stood proud, towering like twisted trees. Shadows and warmth ensconced them as she curtained her pristine wings around them.

He cupped her head between his hands and drew her toward him. He tenderly ran his tongue along where the now healed wound had sliced itself down her skull and bisected her face. It was gone, replaced by flawless white flesh.

A soft sigh escaped her lips. Her hands went over his as she savored this simple, blissful moment. She would continue her chaos, it was natural. Yet she would lessen it, at least in Egypt, for him.

Anup cradled her face. "You are once again whole. As you were before you were harmed. The damage is done and gone. Think no more of it. Everything is exactly as it is meant to be, and always was."

But Discordia knew it would never be the same. She would always remember the pain she had endured. She could never return, not with her brother out there. She would become a wandering goddess, causing chaos in nearly all corners of the world. She nuzzled him, her cheek brushing against his snout as she did.

The tenderness with which she nuzzled him made Anup's neck bristle with sensual joy. But he found the strength to gently push her away.

"Go now. Return to Olympus, or wherever you're permitted to be. Wherever makes you happy. Perhaps this is a sort of rebirth." He looked at her with what was almost a grin. "But try to remain good."

"You do know that is nearly impossible," the goddess smirked. Her wings flapped, brushing them with cold air.

Anup watched as Discordia extended her wings and let them carry her upward, beyond the land of the dead, to the land of the living.

Truthfully, he was relieved to be rid of her. The moment he realized the honesty of that sentiment, he felt a rather generous helping of guilt.

He enjoyed having a living figure to tend to, to wash and mend and heal. He had seen so much death that life, even tenuous, was a marvel. To be given the chance to nurture it, engage her strength and help her heal and thrive was a blessing of its own.

He had appreciated her company. She had brought to him a release which he could not recall experiencing before. He felt renewed, rejuvenated.

He felt as if he could carry on with his duties until the sun was no longer ferried across the skies and Egypt turned cold. And it was all due to her touch.

His lips pulled back into an approximation of a smirk and he headed deep into the Underworld, once more ready, even eager, to accept his post and judge the dead.

As Anup held the hearts in his palms, they felt warm, and it seemed to him that his balance-scales shone exceptionally lovely.

Ra rode the solar barge through the Underworld many, many times as Anup worked his way through the crowd. Thousands had lost themselves to the war defending their lives, lands and families. Anup had nothing but care and respect for each extinguished heart of Egypt. For every half-dozen heart of Egypt Anup judged and set in the jars for eternal protection, he encountered a heart of Greece. Bias easily crept into his senses and his care for these hearts was lax. They scarcely rested in the pans of the scales before he snatched them up and unceremoniously tossed them to the beast Ammit to devour them, damning the Grecian soul who carried the heart in life to endure eternity in torment. To be a being of justice was not always to be magnanimous.

Gradually the choking river of souls drained to a thin trickle consisting of still-births and accidents, of ill-health and euthanasia, most of which were Egyptian.

Where were all the spoils of war? The follies

of chaos?

Had Alexander abandoned his assault? Had Ares grown tired? Had Discordia convinced him that Greece was where they should have always been?

Anup looked down the line of waiting souls. Eyes, old and watery, or huge dark eyes never opened in life stared back at him, waiting. Eyes pale and glassy or matte from death. The queue was reasonable. He would not be long. There was a congestion in the path to the Underworld, and he had to find out why.

ACT II

As SETH WAS WELL AWARE, things in his land were askew, such was a result of war. He, for all intents and purposes, agreed with the war. The people of Greece had no right to this land, and the Egyptian people would not simply lay down and die.

But the earthquakes, the inexplicable fire-storms, the paranormal rains of blood. This reeked of chaos.

Yet it was not his personal brand of it.

He first saw the shadow as it presided over the innumerable corpses of Seth's people, which turned his golden sands red and rusty.

The reaping shadow followed Ares and at first, Seth assumed he was merely War's lackey. As he watched, he realized the shadow had no interest in Ares and was only concerned with the carcasses which dribbled behind the bellicose god.

The figure knelt over each one and used his scythe to slice through the invisible membrane which served to keep the soul bound to the claustrophobic bodily prison. Then he extended his wings and the culled soul was engulfed by the black robes of smoke, cotton, bronze and leather

That alone was interesting enough, but when Anup appeared, it became absolutely fascinating.

Seth watched as they slowly circled each other like whorls in a river. He listened as they exchanged words.

"Who are you?" Anup seemed confused and unsure. His red eyes studied the shadow before him, the cloak and wings as black as the fur on his own muzzle. Seth's foxish ears twitched as he listened, himself wondering about the answer.

"I am that which walks behind the bloody," he answered. His voice was raspy, airy with a hint of seduction. There was an endlessness to it, a faint, low-vibration hum almost too low or quiet to hear, just on the edge of sound. To focus on it brought on unease. "And reap the souls sown deep in the mud by War and Chaos and a Judgemental guide for the dead, a psychopomp to their eternity."

Anup narrowed his eyes, and his ears lowered. He was insulted or threatened perhaps. Regardless he took unkind meaning from the winged shadow's words. The shadow lost interest and turned away from Anup. It proceeded to follow Ares who was oblivious to this midnight collector. He produced his scythe and raised it above his head. In a gold arc he brought it down on the corpse. Metal sang a painful note as the scythe was blocked from the corpse by Anup's *Was*-scepter.

Anup stared into the shadow's hood and looked for a gaze to meet but he saw only lifeless, unending emptiness.

The reaper slowly withdrew and brought himself to his full height. His wings, ragged and molting, fanned out and he adjusted the grip on his scythe.

Anup's nostrils flared and his muscles went tight and hard under his fur.

The first strike was too quick for even Seth to follow, but the two dark figures were now locked in weaponized combat. Scythe met scepter, blade met the two-forked base of the staff. Anup was no warrior, and it was comically apparent, but this reaping shadow seemed to move like a petulant infant. All the finesse he used when cleanly slipping souls from their shells was gone and he bashed at Anup's staff with great, impatient fury. Anup managed to deflect the clumsy, fervorous blows with relative ease. Occasionally Anup would slap the scythe's crescent away with the flat of his hand, causing it to pin itself into the dry dirt. He did this more than once and rolled out of the shadow's reach. Anup rolled again, scooping up a bone picked of most its flesh by vultures and scarabs. It was a leg bone of some horse, broken to an atrocious point. He got to his feet and squeezed his fingers around the bone-like sword. His hand sunk against the scraps of sun-bleached, leathery hide that remained on the bone which helped his grip stay tight and firm.

While the shadow struggled to free the scythe from the sand, Seth watched with great interest as Anup stalked the reaper as the jackals did among the graveyards. Anup raised the bone high above his head, the point aimed at the sweet spot just above the wings, below the skull...

In a flurry of feathers, Discordia stood before the reaper, the bone now aimed at her heart. Her wings rose, blocking the struggling shadow from Anup's view. Their wings brushed together, back to back, mirror images of one another.

"He is a being that came from the bonding we had," she said. She looked calm, though her chest rose and fell quickly. This thing was of the both of them, doubtful she would let him perish when he was so new to the world.

Seth never expected to hear such a sweet confession.

Anup glowered at her, the glow in his eyes growing intense, molten. "You cannot be serious," he snarled.

"I am. Completely." She had none of the mischievousness in her eyes that would have been seen if she had been lying or joking.

Anup looked over her shoulder, over her wing, at the shadow who now stood and loomed over them both in silence. He met her gaze again. "You knew of this creature?" he demanded. "And you did not tell me of its existence? Of my role in its creation?" His voice had grown loud and angry, strong enough for Seth to hear him clearly. For a time, Seth believed Anup was about to strike Discordia, but he threw the spear-headed bone aside and his sceptre vanished in a dazzle of golden light.

She had flinched at his loud voice. She

actually looked fearful of Anup. "I figured the being would help lessen the responsibility on your shoulders."

Anup did not look convinced. "So you're saying you did this for me?"

She hesitated. Seth could see her mind swimming for an answer - will it be the truth, a lie, or somewhere in between?

"His creation was not intended, but what he does will help you."

"These souls died on my sands," he argued. "They must be judged by me!" He bared his teeth and Seth smirked. Seth saw a chance, and he was never one to let an opportunity pass him by.

<><><>

Anup was still ranting, having forgotten about the shadow in a definite sense as it had drifted over to a new row of corpses. His rage was propelled by the abstract.

"What you have done spits in the face of the Nine Ennead of Egypt! Of our very cosmogony! Mine and yours alike. You're already on a razor thin line of losing your powers, why sabotage yourself in such a way?"

She flinched, then she glared at him. "It's in my nature. I was not born to follow anyone's rule. And you well know that. I am chaos, I bring disaster wherever I go."

"Have I been wasting my time?" He shot

back. "Can you truly never change? Are you a self-fulfilling prophecy?" He backed off, and lowered his voice, his expression tinged with sadness and disappointment. "I did not want to believe it. Perhaps I was wrong."

"I almost lied. I considered spinning a tale of how I created the reaping shadow as a way to thank you for saving and healing me, for returning my wings and giving me pleasure. I knew deep down it was wrong." She looked at him. "I am trying to change; do you see me causing any more death? I have stopped killing your people. I have stopped unleashing my chaos upon them. I am trying to do as you wish me to. Trying is the best I can give now."

He crossed his arms over his chest and regarded her. "And what of the shadow you have unleashed into the world?" His voice was stern, clear he was not asking a question but rather demanding an answer.

"As I said, I didn't mean for his existence. He spawned from our joined shadows. He takes souls, it will help lessen your work. Guide him to the souls you deem unfit for your judgement."

Anup let out a long breath. "You're healed and whole. You're a mother." He snorted. Did he not say she had the potential of creation? If only he had known then what he knew now, he would have been so much more careful. "So what will you do with yourself now?"

"Leave. I will not return to Olympus, nor will

I stay here. I will find my shadow and take him with me. Neither of us will see you again."

Anup gave a curt nod. "Likely that is the wisest course of action." He gaze softened and the tension in his shoulders eased. "I wish you well, Discordia."

Discordia had already turned her gaze away. She lifted her wings and with one powerful thrash of feathers, she was gone.

Ares walked the battlefields and said nothing. He raised his sword and severed the head of an Egyptian soldier. Blood came up like a fountain and showered back down on the shoulders of the corpse, who still remained standing on his own two feet.

Then, the neck grew swollen and engorged like a serpent feasting on a rat. From the stump protruded the head of a Seth-Animal. All black, his beak-snout curled back in a dark smirk.

"Hello, Ares."

Ares glared at the creature. His sword was ready to slash the head of the Seth-Animal clean off. "What do you want?" He sneered at the being.

"I think we may have something in common. Discordia. She's not listening to you, and she's elbowing in on my job."

"You have a plan to fix this, I'm assuming? If not, you're wasting my time."

Seth gripped the chest of the corpse he wore,

and the human fingers sunk past flesh and bone. He ripped the chest in two, tearing away the human-suit and tossing it aside. "Have you noticed you're being followed?" He asked, glancing over the war god's broad shoulder.

"I've been too busy to care, but I have noticed, yes." The god crossed his thick, muscular arms.

Seth moved and turned Ares to look upon the shadow. They watched as it autonomously collected souls. Seth pointed. "Look closer. Do the wings not look familiar to you? Your sister has been cavorting with Anup. That shadow is the result of their...union." His mouth curled into a wicked smile. "I trust there are those of your ...clan...which would not take kindly to such wanton debauchery."

Ares' face contorted into an grotesque mask of disgust and he let out an angered growl. "That whore will pay for such treachery. But until we find her, this Anup shall pay."

Seth's eyes narrowed as he tented his fingers. "Mmm. Would it not be quicker to just...throw the sheet from their conspiracy? After all, we all have our kings."

"Perhaps, but first they both shall suffer." The god snarled, sneering at the shadow.

"You're not jealous, are you?"

"Why would I be jealous of such a thing?"

Seth rested his arm on Ares' shoulder. "She is your sister, your twin. And she disobeyed you. She ignores your orders and makes a monstrosity with some dog?"

"I am not jealous of that mutt. I will get revenge upon my sister and on that dog. I am sure she would still listen if it hadn't been for him."

"I just want her out of my hair so I can keep doing what I was made to do," Seth said, flatly. "I don't even care that you're killing everyone. People are born, people die, people are born again. It will be interesting to see what the sands do without so many damned footprints in it."

"Well, you shall soon know." He shrugged Seth's hand off. "I have things to do."

"I have no doubt you do. I'll be watching this situation closely, Ares. Do not dissapoint me."

"You should worry about disappointing me." Ares began walking. It was time to go to Olympus. The war had been won, now it was time for the take over everything within Egypt, and there would be certain gods who would see no mercy.

<><><>

It had ended. Alexander the Great had conquered Egypt so completely and had become Pharaoh. He had claimed himself the son of Amun. A laughable notion, but no one would listen to the dog-headed guardian of souls. Anup gave up before even trying to argue his point.

As the power of Greece grew throughout Egypt, her people adopted the customs of the invaders. As more began to pray to the Olympian gods, Zeus' power grew and the constant murmur of priests praying to Anup gradually faded to but a whisper. With this holy balance slipping in his favor, Zeus decreed that the weaker Egyptian gods would submit to the stronger in whatever way he saw fit.

Zeus, like his father before him, swallowed gods whole. He grew terrible ram horns and claimed the role of Amun-Ra. Wesir, who was renamed Osiris, abandoned all pride and fight and allowed Dionysus to pour never-ending streams of wine down his throat. Anup was given the name Anubis by the Greeks.

Hades ruled the Underworld now. The River Styx had engorged its Greek banks and new branches reached like fingers into the Egyptian Underworld. Anup resented having to look upon it.

He was well aware he was a dying god, force to conform, assimilate with their design or be no more. The Olympians gave him a pittance. He was relegated to judging the hearts of lost newborns or infants. Of course all their hearts were pure. It was busy work, and embalming a still-birth or baby who never breathed air was irritating, they were so small, and sometimes half-formed. At the base of his scales, the crocodile-headed Ammit was starved for the hearts of the guilty. Anup could see her ribs poke through her furred and scaled skin. Each thunderstorm set his own fur on edge, as he wondered if the worst had yet to come, and that storm would usher in fresh punishment by Zeus' hand.

Anup was nursing a quiet rage inside, one which needed to find a way out.

He found himself outside of his realm, among newly re-built cities, Alexandria it was now called. He despised it. It sounded too dainty, too weak. The weakness of its name made light of its foundations, built on bloody sands and the bones of his people.

He was not sure why he stood among its columns, just to fuel the fires of cynicism? It was such a trite thing to do.

"What has brought you here?" Discordia was leaning against a column. Her white hair shone in the sun. She looked bored. While Anup had been forced to engage in his drudgery, she had been sewing minor mischief. A wagon in the distance somehow had all four wheels fall off, a cry from afar moaned of a falling stone from a building breaking their foot; pranks played by the goddess to pass the time.

He nearly answered with the truth, 'I do not know', but he thought better of it. "I came to see what has become of the place I once called home. Yourself? You must be revelling in this."

"Not particularly. It's boring here." She sighed and looked at him. "Shouldn't you be judging souls?"

He scoffed and his eyes blazed. "What is there to judge? Your honoured Hades runs his river through my necropolis. I'm given a token of souls.

Babies, the unborn." He pointed an accusing claw at her. "Between the Styx, and your spawn, I am going mad with anger and boredom."

"I am not the only one at fault for his existence," she sneered at him.

He reached out and grabbed her wrist. He pulled her close to his chest and pressed her arm at an uncomfortable angle. "Don't be coy." He snarled down at her. "This is the sort of chaos you live for. You know you find it thrilling. If anything, you've perverted everything I tried to teach you. You've locked me to you in a way which cannot be undone and you're adoring it!"

She let out an annoyed growl. "I am not, you fool! For one who judges souls, you're horrible at judging the truth." She had been trying, and that trying was the cause of her boredom as she barely found enjoyment causing problems anymore. The chaos she could muster was hardly more than a mosquito bite on the world.

"Then destroy it. Prove you mean what you say, destroy it, and all is forgiven."

"I may not have plotted creating him, but I would rather lose you than destroy the one thing which came from me." She sneered, her eyes dark. "I would rather have my horns torn out ten-hundred-thousand times than destroy my child."

He growled then pushed her away. "Have you any idea what is to be locked out of your own home? To be unwelcomed? To no longer belong to the place you once ruled?"

"I am no longer allowed on Olympus," she said. "My brother has rejected and beat me, as you well know. I understand this more than you think."

Anup looked away. He was not in the mood to sympathise with Discordia. He was entitled to his own rage and pain and he needed someone to lash out at. Discordia could go anywhere, why did she insist on further antagonizing him?

"I have been trying to stay out of your way. It was you who wandered out and found me." She turned away and her large wings fanned out, in preparation to fly away.

"NO," he shouted. Reaching out, he grabbed her wings. "You do not get to escape this time." He pulled her back down to earth, pressing her wings and back to his strong body.

"Let go!" She tried to break away from his grip. "You do not wish me to be around, so let go."

Anup did not fully release her, but he did loosen his hold. "I am abandoned. You are exiled. There is no place for you or I."

Her body was still tense, but she didn't try to pull away again. "No, there does not seem to be. And it's doubtful there ever will be again."

"And so," his palms trailed along her stomach, slowly. "What more is there for the pair of us?"

"I truly do not know." She gradually relaxed, her wings tucked behind her now. She closed her eyes, enjoying the feel of his touch. She could almost feel it against her skin, her red toga-dress was so airy and sheer. "All I know is, all we both once knew is gone."

"Not gone," Anup corrected her. "It is still very much there. It is just out of our reach. Barred to us. Forbidden." He let her melt into him and licked her shoulder. He knew of one way to allay the loneliness.

A hand still rested on her stomach as the other reached lower, slipping under the soft skirt of her dress and cupping her sex in his hand. He slid his fingers between her delicate folds and his arousal pressed against her soft, shapely ass. A soft whimper escaped from her. She spread her legs slightly and pushed her hips forward, encouraging his fingers to explore her growing wetness more easily.

"Much is forbidden to us," Discordia pointed out in a voice full of breath but lacking in power. "But it doesn't mean we shouldn't take what is forbidden." As her hips moved encouraging his hands, she pressed back against him and rubbed her ass against his hardened shaft in yearning.

The two of them sank to their knees, the sand making tender, hushed sounds as it shifted beneath them. Discordia was laid on her back while, on his knees, Anup ducked down between her legs. He let his fingers continue to explore, now probing deeper. He nipped at her inner thighs as his hand continued to work, his thumb brushing back and forth over the peak of her mound. After a moment he retracted his hand, licking her wetness from his fingertips. He bowed his head, letting his tongue now dance over her glistening sex. One of her hands rested behind her to help keep her up. The sand was warm between her fingers. She let out a moan, her other hand went and traced the crown of his head. Her palm stroked the shining black fur there as he ran his long tongue over her. He lapped at her, his muzzle nudging through the folds. His nose grazed her clit as his tongue flicked at her entrance. She whimpered.

Anup growled and his teeth closed down on her folds, his tongue running along the flesh trapped therein. He showed her clit the same painful tenderness, toying with the tiny gentle rosebud. His toes dug into the sand and his erection peeked out from his linens.

Her wings spread out, flapping as the sensations intensified. It made sand float around them as they rest upon it. She let out a cry and arched her hips off the ground, pressing more against his snout.

He grunted, his arousal growing painful. It had been since before the city fell when Anup was last able to feel anything other than loneliness or anger and hate. To feel lust and pleasure and yearning was a blessing. The pain of unanswered need was luxurious. The taste and smell of her was maddening. He needed her touch.

Discordia bent forward, the position awkward. Her breasts were pressed against the base of his skull as she grasped his hardened organ in her hand.

She wanted to touch him; this thrilled Anup. After one last pull of her folds with his teeth, he pushed her hand away and lifted his head. He grabbed her hips and rolled her off her back, which she moved with eagerly, her sand-covered ass presented proudly to the sky. He took hold of her wings and pressed against her, his hardened member sliding in the wetness between them. He adjusted slightly and pushed his cock into her womanhood, his grip on her wings pulling her back to him slowly as her depth embraced him. Another moan passed her lips as she felt him enter her. Her fingers dug into the warm golden sands. Her wings fanned out again as he held them at the base.

The sand on her rear scratched against her skin each time Anup bucked forward, his hips meeting her white flesh. This was an amazing new feeling, this position giving way to new sensations. Anup grinded against Discordia's body, pushing her chest into the sand so he'd find new secret places within her, or guiding her with her wings to rock back and forth against his length. He'd grab her hips and force them to sway in circles. He needed this pleasure. It was something to make him feel present, in the moment.

Discordia let out a chorus of cries, savoring the feeling of him within her, how he filled her, touched spots within which no one had ever touched before. It was glorious and it made euphoria pulse through her body.

There was a bright flash and an enraged roar. Anup felt the pounding in every bit of himself and his fur stood on end. They were thrown apart as a bolt of lightning struck the two of them. Discordia was flung away and landed with a skid in the sands while Anup was slammed into a pillar. They had both been so locked within each other they did not notice the black clouds strangle the sun nor the bolts of Zeus which rained down.

Discordia was shaking as she sat up. The bolt had sent a large wave of pain through her. It seemed she had been naive about believing her being sent away from Olympus was enough of a punishment from Zeus.

Anup managed to get to his feet. He looked past the dunes for Discordia. Was she hurt? He saw her, she seemed merely shaken. He started to run to her.

His leg was caught on something and he looked down to see a chain wrapped around his ankle. He took another step and his other ankle was then shackled by a second chain. Two more restrained his wrists and finally a collar constricted itself around his throat.

Discordia's eyes widened at the sight. She stood up, her body screamed in outrage as each movement caused her pain. She trekked over the sand to go to him, only for a bolt of lightening to strike her once again, and it sent her to her knees. Weak, Discordia reached out for Anup. She wanted to remain with him in the bliss they had found within each other.

Anup tried to fight, thrashing against his binds with rage and terror alike, but it was fruitless. His red eyes stared at Discordia as if trying to tell her something, but she could not discern what it could be. Then the chains began to retract and Anup was pulled under the sand and back to the Underworld.

<><><>

A strong, cruel hand closed around Discordia's wrist and yanked her arm back. Knuckles smashed into her cheek and forced her to relent. Ares' familiar grip once again took her hair, her horns, and he started to drag her. Discordia whimpered in pain when he grabbed her still sensitive new horns.

"Look at yourself. Shameful. Disgusting. You dare poison your body by infecting it with the touch of our enemy? Our prey?"

"Perhaps I enjoy such poison, brother," she sneered. Her bare foot slapped against his shin, which was meaty and covered in a leather and bronze shinguard. He did not seem to notice. She was physically weaker than him, but it was still a sign of defiance.

Ares would have laughed if not for his overwhelming anger. "Once again, having your whoring body on display is no match for a warlord.

You're nothing without armor. End your stupid dancing. You're making a fool of yourself."

"I don't care if I am or not. Let me go," she snarled at him. She continued stomping her bare feet on his sandal-covered foot and against his armored shins. She had to find out what had happened to Anup

"You need to learn humility." Ares dragged her into a dark pit which served as an arena for his own personal amusement. He chained her in large room-sized cage with his vicious war dogs. She was bound as he bound them, with a metal collar and chains around her throat.

"If you wish to lie with dogs, then be the bitch you are." The lock slammed in place over the bars and Ares left her alone in the dark, with the savage panting and howling of her cellmates.

The den was dark, but the sound of the ravenous dogs as they battled for scraps and long bleached bones never quieted. It smelled of death and meat and even when the moon shone its beams between the bars there was little light. There was a cauldron filled with water for the hounds to share, and dusty hay for bedding strewn across the floor.

At least my horns remain, she thought bitterly. She curled up in the corner of the cage. One of the hounds came near, sniffed, then began to rip at her wings. She let out a gasp more in shock than pain and kicked the beast away. The dog let out an angry yelp and then began to bite her, clawing at her. Blood dribbled out of her wounds as she fought back. Her hands struggled as she pawed along the ground for some sort of defense. She found a clean, gnawed bone and thrust her hand forward. The bone sunk neatly through the beast's neck with one quick strike. The dog yelped and then fell limp. She pushed it aside and the other hounds began to tear into it, glad to have such a feast. Discordia glared up at the bit of light streaming down from the top of the pit.

In the scant light from the sky high above, Discordia saw her pale nude form was painted slick with blood from the attack. The rest of her flesh was marred with dark swatches of grime. The silver moonlight glittered off the drinking water in the cauldron. She scooted over to the water to wash. She dipped her hands into the basin and cupped water into her curled palms. She wiped her arms, her face, and ran her wet fingers through her dirty hair. It was too little to really feel refreshing, but it helped.

She was about to scoop up more water when the silver on the rippled surface shifted and took in hues of gold and black. Gazing into the pool like a gateway, Discordia saw Anup's shadow, and heard Ares' voice.

"Don't bother to struggle," Ares' voice was distant, muffled by the boundaries of the water. "Those chains were forged by Hephaestus himself. They cannot be broken."

Sand forced itself into Anup's nose, nestled into the pockets of his cheeks, irritated the roots of his fur and pricked at his eyes. The world moved around him in a blur of cream, gold and browns. There was the occasional gemstone shade of water or sky for the briefest of moments, but they fled too quick and he was again pulled down to his realm, his reality. Just as he was beginning to accept that perhaps he could have more than simply his role in the universe, he was brought back to the ashen shades of his underworld.

With a clang, his back hit a pillar. He knew from the pattern of the points of impact it was the pillar to his tall and proud bronze scales. He looked upwards, left and right, and stared at both arms of his towering talisman. He saw the chains were melted to the base of his scales. So, this was to be his punishment for his indiscretions? Forever bound by heavy chains, to dole out justice to tiny forgotten souls which had barely been alive at all. How trite. Anup expected more creativity.

As he tugged at his chains, trying to find weaknesses or oversights, he pondered Discordia. If he was bound to his scales, what punishment did they find suitable for his co-conspirator? She was already exiled, what more could they do to her? Ares could dismember her again and Anup would be unable to save her this time.

It seemed however, that Ares had other activities on his mind. He came to Anup, with the paws of a skinned lioness hugging his wide shoulders. Anup curled his lip in a snarl.

"You like my new cape?" Ares taunted.

Anup took note of the long gashes that marred the once golden fur. The pelt was ragged and thick with dried blood.

"Sekhmet put up a worthy fight," he answered. He would have time to mourn the war-lioness while bound here. "Your crimson warpaint does not hide your wounds as well as you think it does, you Grecian butcher."

Ares' laugh came forth like rocks smashing together. "Still I am the victor," he said.

Anup tugged at his chain.

"Don't bother to struggle," Ares said. "Those chains were forged by Hephaestus himself. They cannot be broken."

"Where is Discordia?" Anup asked. "What sick torment have you inflicted on her this time?"

"You can forget about her," Ares waved a hand to dismiss the very notion of Discord's existence. He looked at Anup again, scrutinizing the chained god. "We all know of your indiscretions. When Seth first came to me with the secret of your bastard shadow, I thought it was one of his tricks. But when I really looked at it, it was undeniable. I, for one, do not blame you, my sister is quite ravishing. All that raw anarchy. The way her white hair becomes a hurricane as she stands in the scorching updraft of a raging fire, the spears at the end of her antlers; how innocent blood seems to rejuvenate her pale skin."

It was Anup now, who stared at Ares. His gaze was perturbed, confused.

"Unless what you think you feel for her is love. Is it love? You cannot possibly be so foolish."

Anup was aware of the quiet, thrumming rumble in his throat as he growled.

"Did she break your heart, Anubis?" Ares taunted.

"Anup," he corrected with venom in his voice. "What if I did say it was love?" He asked. His eyes hardened, challenging the war god.

Again Ares laughed, "then you have wasted it. Neither my sister or I are capable of love. You touch the hearts of the dead, but you throw your own away on a whore who does not need or want it. I cannot decide if it is more poetic or pathetic."

"You're wrong." Anup got to his feet, but the weight of the chains forced him to slouch, his stance bow-legged, his arms heavy at his sides, his shoulders curved and his neck strained. "I've seen her potential. I've seen deeper into her core than you could ever hope to. You've tried so hard to make her your little slave."

"Slave?" Ares spat. "Says the one in chains."

Anup ignored the taunt. "You can't accept that she is her own entity. You even saved her from mortality."

Ares faltered. "How did you know such

things?"

"Because, Discordia is honest with me," Anup said. "Because she knows how it feels to have someone believe she can be more. She does not need to be oppressed by you. All you see is a tool, a lesser being to be used as you see fit."

"And you see potential and deep into her core?" Ares smirked. "Is that what you said?"

"Among other things."

Anup had no chance to react, the chains were far too much a burden; Ares was on him. He was a warrior and easily overpowered Anup who was now on his back. Ares fingers sunk against Anup's eyes; then there was red, pain, blackness.

Anup was loath to scream, to give Ares such satisfaction but the pain was unbearable and the cries tore from his voice with such ferocity that it scorched his throat.

"You will never again see her," Ares' voice was calm but his violence overwhelming. "You will never again look upon her. You have my word. And you will never again poison her mind with thoughts of betterment."

Anup felt Ares ease his weight off. Sand and grit crunched softly as the war god stepped away. Anup lay on his back in the sightless abyss. "You may have chained me and subdued me," his voice was barely a ragged whisper. "Taken my sight. But Discordia will not heel so easily as a dog."

He heard spit and felt the wet lob land on his

temple and muzzle. He blinked away the sand that Ares kicked in his face. Then Anup was alone, with only the ghostly wailing of the nearby Styx for company.

<><><>

Anup's screams rose to the surface in the forms of bubbles in the cauldron and the images were distorted as the water suddenly came to a rolling boil. The bubbles popped and released Anup's cries of pain as his eyes were crushed to jelly and rooted out from their sockets.

Discordia kicked out and her heel hit the cauldron. It spilled over, the clear water rushing along the ground and pushing the dirt and straw to the edges of the den. The dogs shot to their feet and barked, hopping away from the water in a confused pack.

Was the cauldron a scrying bowl? A trick? An accident? Or a form of torment devised by Ares especially for her? Was it possible what she saw was the future? Perhaps there was still time to stop this from happening. Her wings were still free, she could break the chain. She knew she could. She had to, for Anup.

But she was tired, drained and in pain from the shock of the lightning bolt. Her body was still vibrating in agony. But it did not matter, the pain was fuel, it was motivation. These chains were for dogs, and she was no dog. She was Discordia, the very primordial personification of chaos. Chaos could never be chained. It could never be tamed.

The chains came apart like eggshells in her hands. Her silky black wings spread. She flapped them and launched herself into the air, going up towards the light. Ares was gone, nowhere to be seen around the pit. Perhaps he was still with Anup, or had not yet arrived. She had to stop him, no matter what happened to her.

Ammit, the eater of hearts, had chewed and yanked at the chains. Stedfast, impeccably crafted; they refused to break. Anup could not be certain, but he was reasonably confident that some time had passed. How much, he did not know. Minutes, hours, days? Asleep? Awake?

He tore a strip of cotton from his garments and used it to bind his eyes and staunch the flow of the blood which he had wept. He languished.

More time had passed until he heard a voice which rang off the scales like singing copper blades.

"Hello, old one."

Anup recognized the voice but did not move to acknowledge it.

"Hermes, the great Greek messenger of Olympus. Are you delivering Zeus' apology, or do you have some other message from the mountain? Maybe some mockery." Anup lifted his head to blindly face Hermes.

"Neither. I am here to bring you peace and heal your burning, defiant soul."

Anup forced himself to sit up, he could still cultivate a shred of dignity.

Hermes continued to speak, "The people of Alexandria have adjudicated that you and I are to be merged like the rest of your unworthy pantheon already has."

Anup was unmoved.

"It only makes sense. We are both guides to souls, and proponents of truth."

"And what have *the people* decided we shall be called? Hermanup? It sounds like Dionysus' vomit. Anupherm? Scarcely an improvement."

"Hermanubis."

There was an uncomfortably long span of silence as Anup privately pondered how ludicrous the mangled name was.

"Now," Hermes began, "let us proceed."

"If I refuse?"

"You can try," Hermes said with little concern. "But you will not succeed."

"I will fight you."

"You are weak, Anubis. You will fight, you will weaken even further. You will fade away until you are nothing and I will be the only one remaining. All my teachings and traits will overshadow your memory and all that will remain of you will be your outer shell, which I alone will be wearing. And you will be but a sigh in the back of my throat."

The captive god was silent once more until he finally said, "Anup."

Hermes paid no heed to Anup's tedious inflexibility. "Or, we could work together, as one, in harmony and continue a prosperous existence. You'd be freed, since you would be me and I would be you. You'd regain your sight."

Anup could hear Hermes step closer and felt his hand on his furry shoulder. "We could do great things for our people. The people of Alexandria, the people of Egypt. For they are truly *our* people. And we are their god."

A rod, slender and curved was placed Anup's hands. His hands groped along the rod, feeling its intricately sculpted nature, its cool bronze surface, the slender serpent bodies coiled around the shaft of the stick. Hermes' caduceus.

"No!" Anup threw the caduceus away as if the serpents had come alive and struck his fingers. He shrugged the hands from his fur and tried to scramble away. The sand was turned to mud by his blood and he sunk deeper into the ground beneath him. He felt Hermes' hands grab him by the shoulders and Anup was slammed onto his back.

"Anubis, do not struggle," Hermes said close to his ear. "You are unwell. All of Egypt is unwell." His voice was soothing, placating. A voice made for easing the fear and pain of the sick, the weak, and the frightened. It was alluring, but Anup refused to be swayed. "This will make things better."

"Leave me be!" Anup hollered as he struggled, but hands were on his chest and he could not fight back. The caduceus was pressed back into his palm.

Hermes seemed to sink into his body, and Anup could not resist it. Anup felt possessed, as if the place where his will and soul were meant to be was occupied by something else, as if he was being pushed out of his own flesh.

He was losing himself, and it terrified him. Hermes' memories were supplanting his own, rewriting them with the Olympian's own experience and history. Anup could remember stealing Apollo's sheep but he knew that was implicitly wrong. He recalled presenting a lyre to Wesir after bring him to Duat. The Styx had always been the pulse of Duat and Olympus had always towered over the pyramids.

Whatever Hermes seemed to dislike, he dislodged. Anup's family tree was uprooted and new branches were grafted to it. He could not recall his parents, though he had a suspicion it was Nebt-het and Zeus, a notion that filled him with rage. He knew it was intrinsically false.

With great, tenacious concentration, Anup denied the memories, and Hermes inside him, like an infection. His memories and thoughts calmed and became his own again, and he felt Hermes struggle against Anup's wavering willpower.

His feet itched. He sat up and brought his knees to his chest. His nails dug under the fetters to scratch at the irritating prickle covering his ankles. Spreading out through his matted fur was the soft down of new wings, and the pinprick of feather quills. In retaliation to Anup's fussing, the wings sprouted with violent confidence. They were fully formed and they flapped in anger to which Anup kicked at the air. His legs were brought aloft by the desperate wings and he was dragged along the sand until the chain at his collar grew taught. He reached and grabbed the chain and the manacles slid down and bound the wings to his calves. His legs dropped and he twisted his body, closing his jaws and fists around the wings and ripped them out from his legs. Blood splashed onto the sand and bones crunched in his teeth while feathers tickled his nose and throat. As his strong jaws ripped the wings from his ankles, he lost another piece of himself. The accidental winged shadow he had helped spawn was plucked from his memory like so many molting feathers.

He swallowed, he spat, he sneezed and snuffled. He shook his head frantically to still and quiet the wings. He spat blood and pinions and down.

Anup sat up and his hand touched the caduceus. He took it in both hands and pressed down. The sound of it snapping and the sudden fall of his arms as it came apart was quite satisfying. The satisfaction died a moment later as the two ends came together, attracted to one another the way magnets would be, and it was once again whole.

Anup smashed it over his knee and tossed one end away. Far away, there was a splash and the horrified wails of old souls. It had fallen into the Styx. But the staff's weight shifted and he knew it had mended itself, growing like a lizard's severed tail.

Anup reached down and grabbed it, smashed it again and again, gnawing, twisting, kicking, crushing it over his own skull and shoulders, bending it with his teeth, playing tug of war with Ammit, but it would not stay broken for long. His efforts had to pause every few minutes so he could rip and chew fresh feathers from his feet.

"Anup..." The gentle swish of wings folding was heard after she landed. He felt her soft hands touching his snout when he moved his mouth from his bloody ankles. He could not smell her, he could smell only his own blood.

He recoiled from her touch at first. "Discordia? No, you are not here." He shook his head and her hands slipped from his cheeks. "I am going mad. You're a delusion. Nothing more. A delusion or a deception."

Discordia ignored his objections. "I came too late. I'm sorry." She cradled his head against her breast. His arms went around her and he embraced her, his body leaning like lead into hers.

"Delusion or not," he said, "stay."

She pressed her lips to the top of his head. "I am no delusion, Anup. I will not leave." She lifted his face upward with her hand. "But it is not too late. I could heal your eyes, as you had for my wings. You just have to instruct me."

It was a realistic plan, but a crushing blow came seconds later. He leaned into her touch and sighed. "It will not matter," he shook his head softly. "Very soon my strength will wane and I will stop being me." He gestured to the wings once again itching and growing from his ankles, "and will become whatever abomination Olympus wants me to be."

He held her tight and Discordia could felt him tremble. "This cannot be," she whispered, seemingly to herself.

"It is not enough they take our land and slaughter our people, but now they wish to make us one in the same. To eliminate us completely." He said, morose and miserable. "Ares has claimed war and killed Sekhmet, and I..." His voice trailed off as he started scratching at his ankle with his toes. He could feel, *hear* Hermes inside him, telling him it was Anup's duty to conform to his role, that it would be best for the people. He could feel his sense of self weaken, fade. "I should hate you for what your gods have done to us..."

"Remember, I stopped taking part in what they have done long ago." Still cradling his head, Discordia's fingers speared through his dirty and bloody fur.

He shook his head once, gravely, and pressed his brow against her full, naked breasts. "I don't care.

Egypt is no more, the Heliopolis is just another lesser Olympus, and Duat," he fell silent. "I can scarcely remember what it looked like before the flooding of the Styx. It does not matter. Things are changing and there is nothing to be done about it."

"It was a beautiful place," she said softly. "I hoped I would have been able to save you, so that you would not change from the proud being you had been." Her voice was thick with sorrow.

Anup took note of her use of past-tense. He still trembled and scratched while in her arms. Blood was still all he could smell. He cuddled more into Discordia's warmth and softness but with every movement he made, he could hear his chains rattle like a taunt, a lesson, berating his thoughts and actions.

"I have need for you, Discordia."

"I will do anything for you, Anup." She pressed her lips to the blood matted fur on his snout. She could not break his chains, but she could give him reprieve from the pain. Pleasure was the only thing she could give.

Anup lifted his arms to embrace her, but the chains denied him. His shoulders sank and he pulled away, falling heavily against the pillar of his scales. He would have looked at her if he could see, but he drew his face to the direction of her voice.

"Destroy me..." He said quietly. "Before he succeeds in melting and burning away all that I am." He gestured to his feet. "And claims me completely."

She sighed, "I cannot do such a thing. But I can make you forget the pain, and live in the now." He was one of the few she could not stomach destroying. She laid him back, her hands running through his dirty fur, missing the silkyness of it. She straddled him, kissing along his snout. The way she touched him seemed loving.

He seemed reluctant but he lay back, the best his chains would let him. "You can," he said. "But you will not. Why is that? Are you afraid? I thought you enjoyed misery and chaos."

She turned her head away, not that he could see. "I do, but I cannot destroy you. If I lose you..." she shook her head and moved her hands along his body, choosing to be silent now. She couldn't describe her feelings, she doubted she ever could.

So she would have him suffer. A truly selfish choice on her behalf. Could she not see that she would soon lose him anyway? Well, if he could not have death at her hand, he could at least accept what she was offering. His hands came up and his palms cupped her breasts, his fingers leaving trails of blood as he fondled her. He sat up and she slid down his stomach, onto his lap. "It would be easy," he said to her. "Get a knife. Strike me right here." He spread her breasts and licked between them. "Quick and clean. No more suffering."

The touch of his tongue against her warm, hidden skin sent shivers through her body. Her hand slid between them, cupping his cock. "I couldn't. I would rather become mortal than to lose you." She hated admitting so, but it was true. After all, to her becoming mortal was a fate worse than any other.

It occurred to him perhaps she heard what she had told her brother, but how? Regardless, it didn't really matter.

He rested his head on her chest. "...Then please..." His voice was so very tired. "Assuage my pain."

Discordia leaned her brow on top of his head and he felt his fur dampen slightly from her tears. Her hand slipped beneath the cloth covering him and she began rubbing his length. He let out a small groan as her hand slid along him. It took time, longer than usual, but gradually the pain and itching was overtaken by arousal.

She kissed his nose as her hand moved away. She pulled his clothing free and set it aside, and let her sex press against his. She rocked her hips and slid back and forth along the underside of his shaft, forcing his cock to press against his belly. He could feel her damp slit as it dragged against his thick manhood. Discordia let out a small moan.

Though he was without sight, Anup knew Discordia's body well. He reached up and the chains sung in his ears. His hands curled around her antlers and he pulled her head to him. He kissed her, his length yearning to be buried inside her.

She returned the kiss, her hand grabbed his cock at the base and guided him into her. The now familiar sensation of him slipping inside caused her to moan against his mouth.

Anup let go of her antlers and cradled her head in his hands, her long, soft hair threaded its way around his fingers and mingled with his fur.

Her hands covered his and she closed her eyes as her hips danced against him. She let out a soft moan at the sensations. It felt like an eternity had passed since they had been together.

Anup leaned forward, straining against his bonds, lowering Discordia to her back. His chains complained and kept his arms restricted so he was unable to put his hands on the ground, or even on her. He growled in aggravation and yanked his arms forward, forcing the kinked-up links in the chains to align and earning himself some slack.

Her arms slipped around him while her wings fanned out on the ground beneath her. With each thrust into her, Discordia moaned, her hips moving to meet his.

He had to be satisfied with an awkward semi-crouched position. His toes spread into the bloody sand as he struggled to find purchase. The chains, the discomfort, the itch, it was all so maddening. Fresh blood seemed to weep from his eyes and pat softly onto the sand. His toes continued to dig in an effort to find stability but none came. The muscles in his feet tensed. But Anup would not rage, he'd just let it flow through his muscles, and give it to the sand and blood.

As the fires of their lust continued, the blood beneath them seemed to seep aside and tighten, solidify. The puddle of mud and blood oozed and gathered and rose up. It pulled itself from the sand, through the puddle, and walked. The being was red, and difficult to describe. It seemed to possess a white-hot core where a heart should be, its figure red and jagged, sharp and cutting. Wrath personified, given form and shape.

Discordia's legs went around Anup's hips, offering a small bit of support. She pressed her lips to his mouth, her fingers slipping through his bloody fur.

He licked her lips and she could taste feathers and blood. He knelt on his shins and held her close, rocking under her as he nuzzled his head to her neck. He could smell her now, her sweat and natural scent embedded in her hair and wings, the musk of her scent energizing him further.

"Please…" he said between cuddles and thrusts. "Just slit my throat. Then it is over. You're absolved and I am at peace. Please."

Selfish, his request was selfish. Greedy. And so too was her refusal.

Rage coursed through her veins. "No. I cannot!" Of course she still wanted him here. She felt lust for him, among other things. She would not allow herself to be the one to end him.

"You can," he said. "It's what is best for both of us." He shuddered, a thrill rolling weakly through his body. "Cut me, choke me. They've already broken me. You would be putting me to rest."

"I couldn't, even if I wanted too." She whimpered beneath him, despite what he asked of her, she still found pleasure from being with him.

As Discordia continued to deny his request, Anup felt a strange sense of abandonment. He released her and pushed her off. If she was to reject him, then he too could reject her. She fell into the mud ass-first and her wings flapped angrily when she hit the ground. His ankles itched as new feathers sprouted. He focused for a moment, strengthening his control over Hermes as the internal struggle waged. Anup was unsure how long his control could last, but did not wish to waste this time. His nails clawed at the new wings and dug trenches into his legs. The reprieve ravishment brought him had faded. He reached out, his hand searching blindly through dead space before he found her body again. He dragged her through the mud to him. Her wings continued to flap and made it a little bit harder to bring her back to him. Eventually her body was pressed against his again.

Somewhere in her struggles, Discordia had flipped onto her hands and knees. He felt the curve of her ass against his hips, and it was slippery with mud. His cock slid between her thighs, the head rubbing against her belly. She shuddered, she couldn't help but feel joy just by having his length pressed against her body. Her wings folded behind her back, and her small struggle ended. Lust surged throughout her body, bringing a sort of warmth within her. It flowed around her, reaching the very tips of her wings before it seemed to seep out of her, it wasn't the same way the pleasure usually flowed throughout her body. She mentally shrugged it off as it seemed to pool beneath her.

Her eyes shut and she focused on the thrilling hum of her body, the lust that flowed through her. As her attentions turned to the wild feelings inside her, the pool of liquid beneath them began to flow away unnoticed, like a river of molten gold. It stopped within the shadows and as the last drop entered into the pool, began to mold into the shape of a woman.

Her hair was a silky black that resembled Anup's fur and pale blue eyes to match Discordia's. Her skin was a golden tan and her body flawless. She stood aside, watching the two together with a smirk on her face.

Anup slid along her like they were made of ice, her heat melting the space between them. His groans matched Discordia's moans as she easily took all of him deep, feeling the tip of him brush against the limit of her depth. His hand went up her ribs and he cradled her breasts in his palms, squeezing the soft, plush swells of flesh, pressing her hardened nipples between his fingers. His hands sunk into her breasts and they bounced in his palms with every thrust. He ran his tongue along her back, tasting mud and blood and chaos. This was how they were when Zeus had blown them apart. It was only fitting they reclaim this position.

He leaned forward and his tongue tasted her antler. "Pierce my heart with one of these," he murmured. "I never intended for any of this." His voice was by her ear, shuttering with each thrust. "But I need you. I need this. Peace...Bring me peace, Discordia, please."

He heard a sound, like a sob. Discordia had never cried, not in his presence at least. "If I were to kill you, then how would I join you?" One of her hands rested over his.

He embraced her, his strong arms wrapping around, crossing over her breasts and he rested his cheek on her back, between the spot where her wings sprouted.

"You're determined. You'll find your way to me."

She squeezed her eyes shut. "Just give me this last time and I will do it." She finally whispered as her tears mingled with the mud, blood and sand.

"One...last time." He repeated. "One last bout of pleasure."

"Yes..." She leaned her head back to nuzzle him.

He took hold of her and reared back, holding her to his chest. Her legs spread as she straddled his thighs. She reached back to grip the scruff of fur at the base of his skull and he gave the side of her neck a lick. He kept her close with one arm, while his fingers of his other hand danced along her clit and coaxed music from her throat. Her moans and cries of delight echoed around them. Her hips jerked and rocked against his as he toyed with her. He felt her tremble on him as her legs worked along his to impale herself repeatedly on his shaft. Her nails scraped the back of his neck as she moved on top of him. If there was anything within the afterlife for gods, this would be the one thing she would remember most there, being with him like this.

He squeezed her tight around the ribs and pinched her between his fingers as his first climax of their last time hit him and Discordia felt a rush of electric fire draining from him and filling her.

Discordia cried out as he filled her, her body shuddered and tightened as her own release soon followed. She shook slightly from the joy of such a blissful release. Her hands, still resting on the back of his neck, began to move and stroked his dirty and matted fur.

Anup kissed and nipped her neck. The last time. It was to be the last time.

One more time.

Discordia moved off him, only to turn and gently push him onto the ground. Though he could not see her, she wished to face him, to kiss him and savor their final moments together.

Anup felt the wet, soft, feather-covered sand against his back. He reached up and touched her face, his thumbs lightly stroking her eyelids, her nose, her lips. His fingers traced the curve and shell of her ears and her hair spilled over her shoulders and shrouded his knuckles. When his hand touched her lip again, he felt it move into a sad smile. His hips arched under her as he tried to recall the last time he looked into her eyes, and what colour they had been.

She missed his eyes, neither of them could look into the other's eyes again. Her hands ran along his chest, favouring the feel of his fur. It hadn't the same silkiness as before, but she still loved the sensation.

As the lovers went on, they released more of their troubles into the sand. A trio of thick, slow, fat-gutted figures, one with four arms and a miser's face, another with the bloated pocketed cheeks of a rodent, and the third with the lazy body of a slug, rose from the sand and bumbled away as had the golden girl from before. Greed, Gluttony and Sloth. The golden girl and the raging red figure now had brothers. Soon they found their path blocked by the Styx. The triplets looked at eachother, grinned with sharp teeth, and drank deep.

Anup wanted to tell her, to confess, that no matter what happened, he was grateful. He felt more with her than he had for centuries. For better or worse she made his existence lively, colourful. But if he lay down such sentiment, she'd likely refuse to do him in. So he said nothing.

She wished she had the power to free them

both but his chains were unbreakable. If things had been different, they could have been so much more together. If they had made an attempt of escape sooner, they could have been free rather than taking their last moments of passion together, savouring all they could.

One by one they let go of the dark parts. The rage, the pride, the envy, the apathy, but they reveled in others; the greed, the lust, the gluttony, entwining into and around each other in various positions, exploiting every second of their situation and coercing the rapture from it. Finding new excuses not to let it end. New ways to be together, new places to stimulate, new parts of themselves to explore.

She nuzzled him as they lay on the ground, catching their breath between their lust-filled moments.

Anup felt a beautiful weightlessness and a tingling throughout his entire body. He felt no itch, no pain, nothing but his cheek against the perfect softness of Discordia's hot skin.

Two more figures pulled themselves from the stink and glow of the god's ecstasy. The two were similar, but not. Satisfaction for the rules they broke and the vivacity that Anup and Discordia shared gave them life. Personification of their pride, and the envy toward their brethren who could indulge in relations without being punished.

The beautiful feeling of their bond made

Discordia sigh in contentment. Even with all that was happening to the both of them, she would not trade this blissful moment for anything.

Despite his blindfold, he moved his head to look at her. His blindness did not concern him, the lesser god trying to possess him did not concern him, the fact these were to be their final moments together. None of it mattered. He simply did not care.

With his brazen damning of it all, their final spawn came into this world, a run-off of what remained, the heavy ball of hopelessness. It was dry and steely and a weight to bear. And they cast off that weight, that sense of duty, for these precious seconds of happiness.

Apathy was unmoved, a stone which rose from the sand and was cooled by their shadows, it would not be compelled. It remained, as Lust and Greed gave in to each other, as Sloth and Gluttony drank the souls from the Styx and as Envy admired Pride while Wrath screamed for release, Anup held on to Discordia one moment more.

"You gave me your word."

A tear slid down her cheek. "I did. I will keep my word to you." She kissed him, one more kiss as she steeled herself for what was to be done.

Anup tasted her kiss and he squeezed her arms. "Do not weep," he said. "I cannot tolerate the thought that my attention has made you weak." He got to his feet and pulled Discordia up with him.

She nuzzled him, she wished it hadn't ended so soon but she had to keep her promise. She wanted to leave him with one thought before his life ended. "I love you," she whispered in his ear before she moved her head from his and he felt her antlers plunge into his heart.

Anup let out a sputtering cough and he grabbed her horns. He pulled, and jammed them deeper into his body resulting in a thorough impalement. He let her go, and cradled her head to his chest. He could feel his blood seep from his wounds and colour her hair.

"You do me a great service," he whispered. Discordia could hear the life draining from him as his voice slipped quieter and quieter. "You are a goddess of mercy." He eased back, pulling himself from her antlers. The velvet on them rubbed his wounds raw and made them burn. Anup fell to his knees.

It was then Discordia noticed the long black feather in his fingers, plucked from her wing.

"A souvenir," he had said then, as he did now. Discordia was instantly brought back to that day. It felt like it had been forever when it had truly only been such a short time ago. Her fingers combed through the fur on his head.

"Keep that. Even when you pass on to wherever you go." She kissed his forehead, "I want to be with you, always."

He lifted his head to her. "I was not wrong,"

he whispered. "I knew you had the nurturing side of you. Discordia, you are a creature of many facets. Good. Evil. Creation. Destruction. Mercy and spite. But I now see it was wrong to try and pull the parts which served me best out of you. It took forced conversion and unwillful submission before I understood. You are Discordia. You are chaos. You are not the meek and demure thing I tried to coerce you to be. Be what you've always been believed to be. Just be honest, and cut your own path. Others be damned."

There was a gentle blast of wind and the sands rose through the air, turning Discordia's vision yellow-white. It lasted a moment or two before the sands fell, rested and settled.

Anup was gone.

ACT III

SHE DUG HER HANDS into the sand he had once laid upon. She squeezed her eyes shut, holding in the tears. He was gone from her. She would embrace who she was, ruin as much as she could before the gods stopped her. She wanted to unleash every feeling she had on the world for what she had lost and gained.

Discordia lay in the discoloured puddle of bloodied sand and let her mind drift across all the possible ways to descend her fury among the other gods. Her hands took fist-fulls of sand and she held them to her breast. The final thing Anup left her, it still smelled of him.

She lay for hours, in a near catatonic state. Like the tide, her palm smoothed out the sand until the surface was flat. Then she began to run her fingers through the level sand, dragging patterns out of it and forming images not unlike the pictures which adorned a pharaoh's tomb. She drew him, her index finger stroking his grainy cheek and his illustrated ears were tall and proud. But Discordia was no artist, and the image was out of proportion, askew, and completely wrong.

The eight newborns gathered around her and watched the image develop as Discordia etched it into the sand.

Discordia looked around and saw her

children. They were all vastly different but each one retained a hint of Anup. None more so than Envy, a wiry man-dog hybrid with fur the colour of palm-leaves and poison. Mangey, barrel-chested and sunken stomached, his eyes were also a sickly green. He looked longingly at Pride.

Pride looked not unlike Discordia, though her black hair shimmered like the rainbow of an oil-slick. Her wings were much larger and grander than Discordia's, and the feathers not black, but airy, colourful peacock tail feathers. Useless for flight, but beautiful and unique. She knelt by Discordia and mimicked her finger movements in the sand, but had interest in drawing only herself.

Four-armed Greed clung to golden-skinned Lust from behind, claiming her as his own. Lust laughed, her dark hair spilling over her shoulder as she pressed her rump against his lap, because it amused her.

Sloth dozed, leaning heavily against soft, squishy Gluttony. Wrath stewed, simmering, waiting for a chance to explode. Apathy was in a state of hopeless catatonia, as Discordia had been moments ago.

Discordia's eyes, red with sadness and anger, fell upon one of her creations. Wrath...This child of theirs could aid her.

"Come, my son. I have a way for you to unleash yourself." She stood.

Wrath looked at her, a figure of only blood

and fire and a little bit of bile. Sometimes the exposed cord of muscle was seen under the scorched, fluidic coating. He said nothing, but followed Discordia, leaving a trail of burnt and broken earth behind him.

"Want to come," Envy said, and he galumphed behind the two. Lust shrugged Greed off and trailed after them, while Greed decided there may be more treasures to find wherever the others were going. Gluttony, under the same thoughts of Greed, dragged Sloth and Apathy behind him as he took up the rear. Pride looked up from her drawing and hurried after, pushing her way through the parade until she was shoulder to shoulder with Wrath and Discordia.

"We are going to take down Olympus. We are creatures not meant to follow the rules." Discordia stated, "And so, we shall bring down what will try to stop us, my children. Their rules took your father and for that we must take their precious rules from them." Discordia stood tall, proud. Once again she was the flash of chaos Anup had tried to change her from. She was back and she would not allow her brother to control her chaos this time.

Discordia had an army, one born from her own flesh and blood and soul. Anup was correct. He had been correct all along. She was a being of creation.

But she always enjoyed destruction more.

Setting foot on Olympus was the right of any Grecian God, thus Discordia and her army did so, appearing in an instant there together, stepping on the cool marble floor before Zeus and Hera on their thrones. Discordia stared defiantly at the two. "Your rule has come to an end. Chaos shall reign now."

Her children --Superbia the Prideful, Tristitia the Hopeless, Avaritia the Greedy, Luxuria the Lustful, Invidia the Envious, Gula the Gluttonous, Ira the Wrathful and Acedia the Slothful, the Staligia-- stood behind her with their heads raised.

"Where did these abominations come from?" Zeus demanded. Ira objected to the slander with a bubbling hiss.

"Nice place you have," Invidia quipped with a nervous tick. "I think I'd like the throne most of all," he stepped forward, but Superbia stepped forward first.

"We are your better. Stand down and relinquish all that is yours, you inferior insects. This needn't be bloody."

"Sure it does." Ira hissed, licking his lathered jaws.

"Oh, it will become very bloody if they do not give us what we want." Discordia turned from her children and spoke to Zeus. "I don't like the way you run things. It's about time for a change, Isn't that right, my children?" She walked around the throne, she seemed untouchable. Upon the earth fire rained down and disasters whirled, one after another. The mortals were thrown into horrible chaos.

Luxuria smiled softly and walked even softer through the crowd of her siblings. Her breasts bounced slightly with each step, and her hips had a far too-perfect sway to them. She was unlike anything Aphrodite or Eros could ever provide, a million pleasing, filthy broken promises. "Oh, noble rulers of Olympus. I am not one for violence. I'm sure we can come to a conclusion to please us all, if given enough time to work through our differences." Luxuria was the first who managed to get to the thrones, and she took Zeus' hands, coaxing him to his feet. "Come with me, King."

As Luxuria the Lustful guided Zeus toward his bedchamber, she locked eyes with her mother. Both women were well aware of Zeus' own lecherous ways. The newborn woman and the entranced king of Olympus crossed the court and before Hera could protest her husband's philandering habits, Superbia the Prideful had her pinned to her throne.

"You did not listen. I am your better. Even my pathetic slothenly brother is your better!"

"Oh, she is far from our better." Discordia agreed with her daughter and plucked a strand of hair from Hera's head. "I never did like your hair. Perhaps I should take it off. But just a cut would be boring." She turned toward Ira. "Would you do the honor of setting her on fire, my son? It would be fun to watch someone so high and mighty burn."

Ira's face contorted into a frightening impression of a smile, bloodthirsty and wild. Burning blood dripped from his teeth and sizzled on the marble. He stalked up to the throne, and Superbia and Discordia gave him room lest they be caught in his rampage. He slapped his palm down on Hera's scalp and gripped her head. It smouldered and bubbled, the flesh growing waxy and greasy. As the heat rose, Hera's struggles grew and soon she was screaming and writhing where she sat. Then, she was wearing a crown of flames, her beautiful hair a melted, charred veil down her back and shoulders.

Discordia purred. "Much prettier this way, don't you agree, Hera?" She sneered down at the woman. "Hmm, still not pretty enough. Her eyes ruin the look. My dear son, I trust you'll make her a glorious vision to show what your power can do." She left Ira to Hera. "Take what you will, my children. Burn and maim all who get in the way of your fun!"

Her wings flared out and her children knew it was time to spread out and play. To steal the treasures of the gods and destroy what they had built their ancient kingdom on.

It was a complete carnage, though nothing they did caused any god to actually expire. Discordia wanted them to bear witness to her rule. Through months, years, Discordia and her Staligia meticulously reduced the Greacen gods to their most base elements. They were rendered to drooling, screaming or crying ghosts of themselves. Luxuria easily exhausted Aphrodite, Eros and even the extremely virile Zeus himself. Acedia the Slothful and Tristitia the Hopeless effortlessly brought Athena's wisdom to its knees through sheer carelessness and malaise. Avaritia the Greedy and Gula the Gluttonous tore open Dionysus and got drunk on his wine as they drank it directly from the god's bloated stomach.

While Discordia turned Olympus into her personal orgy of insanity and torment, Ares was nowhere to be seen. But now he stormed the mountain on his chariot that was drawn by the very war hounds that had mauled his sister in his cage. He would take back Olympus, perhaps even keep it for himself and crown himself king.

There was a clash of meat and bone as Discordia's little boys savaged the dogs before Ares even had a chance to dismount. He jumped over the carnage and landed on the marble floor. His sword was drawn and he launched himself at Discordia with a bloodthirsty battle cry.

Ira crashed into him, abandoning the squealing dogs and pounded both fiery fists into Ares' chest. He grabbed the blade of the sword and twisted but Ares would not relent his hold. Ira twisted again and slammed the pommel, and Ares' stoney fist, directly against Ares' teeth. Some of them shattered like glass and blood poured forth like a sweet oasis. Ira let him go and hissed, expecting Ares to rise and engage in battle.

Ares looked around and saw Avaritia, Invidia, and Gula dining upon his prized hounds while Superbia draped herself in the most full and pure of their furs. His hand was mangled and his sword was in splinters like shattered pottery. He looked back at Ira, then his broken sword. The others had their fill of the hounds and were now turning their attention on their uncle.

Ares realized he could not defeat Ira the Wrathful in combat, nor his bastard kin. Honor was not in their nature and something more primal than his godly power surged through their veins. This was a war he could not win head on; he would have to strategize.

Ares snapped to his feet and launched himself from the throne room and down the mountain. He slid on the soles of his sandals, running the leather raw as he rushed down as if he were molten lava flowing down a volcano, destroying all in his path.

"After him, my son," Discordia yawned against the back of her hand as she spoke to Ira. "I wish for my cowardly brother to be chained and muzzled, prostrate before this throne, watching helplessly as we rule the other gods." She looked to her prideful daughter. "You. I have a task for you, as well. Find me the one called Seth and bring him to me. He needs to see what true chaos is, with his own eyes."

Superbia smirked, having been chosen for such an important task boosted her already inflated ego. She vanished, going to Egypt to search out Seth.

Discordia sat back and waited. Merely the anticipation was enough to please her. For the moment.

Ira the Wrathful had little trouble tracking Ares. War was seldom a subtle creature and Ira could smell blood anytime, anywhere. Hunting Ares was like tracking a wounded animal. He found Ares just outside of a now massacred village in the mountains. The smell of blood was thick in the air.

Ira's mouth filled with saliva and blood streamed from his gums onto his tongue. He rushed to the ruin, turned a corner and his body slammed into Ares' back like a boulder. Ares flew forward, landing on the dirty ground. He let out an angry growl.

"How dare you touch me, you filthy creature." He stood, his muscles flexing with effort as he did. The earlier battle had left him weaker than he typically was. Blood flowed from his broken teeth and nose, and coloured his black beard.

Ira said nothing, or perhaps he did, but it was all just a garbled cacophony of screams and wails of pain and anger and hate. Different from the screams of victims of war, those were sad, or proud. Ira's voice was only the rage of bloody fumes and shattered bones.

Ares couldn't stand the sound, unsheathing his dagger, he pointed it at Ira. "Silence!" He demanded, his ears ringing from the wails of pain and hate.

Ira did not quiet or become still. He lunged again, barrelling into Ares, caring not for the threat of the dagger. They grappled one another. Ira clawed at Ares and tore Sekmet's skin from his shoulders.

Ares punched and tried to use his blade, but the weapon was useless in this battle. He let out an angry yell, how could he be beaten by such a vile thing?

Ira's maw opened, his jaw unhinging like a snake's. He breathed in Ares' screams and drank down his rage, swallowing it deep into his pit of his stomach and letting it burn his heart. Ira grabbed the spiralled horns of Ares' helmet and ripped it from his skull, nearly pulling Ares' head off the neck.

Ares couldn't help but to yell in pain. He was not meant to lose, not to this being.

Ira grabbed Ares by the neck and continued to sup on the war god's cries. Ira felt strange sensations moving through his body as he fed on Ares' agony and rage but was too simple minded to be able to identify the feelings as pleasure, giddiness.

Ira pulled back his arm as he clutched the helmet and cracked it right into Ares' face. A ram horn crashed into his temple and Ares saw stars. Ira swung again with a back-hand motion and struck the other side of Ares' head. Back and forth, back and forth, Ares' head was batted at, like a cat toying with a mouse. Blood spattered from his mouth, he let out pained noises at each blow. He was defenseless and he hated it. He was a war god and he was being reduced to a bloody pulp. His remaining teeth flew from his jaw and into Ira's mouth. They were crunched to dust and swallowed down along with the rest of Ares' misery.

Ira finally stopped, because he knew if he continued, Ares would be obliterated and his mother had been very specific. Bring him back to her alive.

Superbia the Prideful was just outside of a Temple of Seth in the centre of a place called Ombos. She was not going to waste time hunting the chaotic charlitain. She did not operate in such ways. She was too good for it. She would make him come to her.

She walked into the temple, running her fingers over the gritty, painted walls. She inhaled the musty air, thick with sand that caught between a person's grinding teeth. She rolled the granules on her tongue ponderously as she perused the carvings and paintings on the wall. Her search ended when she found a particularly regal and well cared for depiction of Seth. She pulled her bronze dagger from her belt and slashed a cut into the stone wall.

She gored the image of Seth, severing his head from his neck. She cut another gash, then another, forming a perfectly scribed "X" across his body. Finally she plunged the blade into the heart of the image.

Seth's laughter filled the chamber. Superbia turned around.

"Laughter?" Superbia said. "I would have thought defacing your image would have brought you rage."

Seth threw his head back and simply continued to laugh. "I'm laughing at you. Your wings. So ridiculously over-blown. Huge, impractical, and incapable of flight."

Her feathers remained unruffled. "Do you mean to mock me? Disarm me with cutting words instead of cutting weapons?"

Seth just let his snickers eventually grow still and silent.

"It won't work. Barbed tongues don't hurt me. Because, quite simply, I am better than you. Say whatever you want about me. I know the truth. It is your jealousy speaking."

"Oh, child," Seth shook his head. "You are not proud. Pride requires grace and honesty. Confidence. What you are is arrogant. You mistake your stubbornness for grace and your accusations of jealousy as honesty. What you think is confidence is merely bluster."

"And for a god of chaos you're tragically

predictable," Superbia lamented. "You should come with me to see my mother. She could show you what a true god of chaos can do."

"You think me a fool? You can't even tell a good lie."

"I do not lie." Superbia said. "Do you fear her? That's probably wise. If not for your interference, the Olympians may never have known about the affair, Anup would still be here, I and my siblings might not, and Discordia wouldn't be blasting the planet away. Or perhaps this is what you wanted? But, I doubt it. There's no satisfaction while someone takes your job from you, and does it better. In fact, I would say it's humiliating." Superbia smiled, a cruel, cutting expression. "What was your idea of chaos again? Kill your brother, usurp his throne and marry his wife? Rule Egypt from one end of the Nile to the other? Such small aspirations, Seth. Discordia has brought Olympus to its knees and chaos reigns all across the new world and old."

As Superbia spoke, Seth could see the barbs on her forked tongue and see the sweet venom which shone on her full lips, making them glossy.

"Such a small man, with small ambitions." The words seemed to buffet at him. They ran over his body like a landslide. He stumbled, bruised.

"Small," she said again and Seth began to feel the futility of arguing her truth. She stood taller and he recoiled from her voice, shrinking back. Her words beat him down until he could fit in the palm of her hand.

She closed her fingers around him.

<><><>

Discordia's two children presented themselves before her. Superbia had the diminutive Seth in a dull brass cage which she offered to her mother. The cage was placed at the foot of the dais.

Ira dragged his beaten and bloody uncle by the ankle and wherever they went they left a trail of blood. He wore Ares' blood-soaked helm askew on his own head. Around his shoulders, Sekhmet's torn skin hugged him. The spoils of War. He threw Ares gracelessly toward his mother and Ares rolled with a groan. Discordia gestured with a hand and Ira grabbed Ares' arms and held them out while Invidia grabbed the captive's ankles. Discordia rose from her throne and stepped with regal confidence down the dais. Superbia approached, holding coils of thick metal chains, each one ending in a cuff. One by one the manacles were locked around Ares wrists and ankles. He soon discovered the cuffs were lined with rows of dagger-sharp spikes, each a mere half-inch long. Four fetters were placed, with one remaining still.

Superbia passed the final chain to Discordia, who held it gingerly in her hand. She stepped up to the bound war god, then stepped on him, directly on his unimpressive manhood. Her toes had to curl to keep balance. Her other foot stepped on his rock-hard warrior's chest and the blood that covered his skin squished between her toes. She knelt and locked the final heavy, biting collar around his neck. The spikes sunk into his meaty neck like crocodile teeth.

Discordia knelt, her lips close to Ares ear, and whispered. "Brother dear, don't bother to struggle. Hephaestus forged these chains especially for you."

<><><>

Discordia sat on the throne. While happy with her winnings, she felt so lonely, even with her precious children. Superbia and Ira were usually by her side, and she would find brief amusement when Ares rattled his chains or Seth gnawed at his bars. The world was in darkness under her rule. She took to wandering the mortal world daily, enjoying the chaos she brought down upon the lands. No mortal could see the goddess. Occasionally she would see her eldest, The Reaper. She did not admit it to the others, but he was the one she favoured the most. She would spend hours shadowing him as he gathered the souls into his cloak. He had, in his years, amassed an impressive collection and was still without a place to put them all. His cloak would shift and writhe from the souls struggling within, but he was stoic and it did not seem to bother him. In fact he seemed aware of very little, save for his duty.

She lifted her head and took in her surroundings. It took a moment for Discordia to realize she was no longer in Greece, but rather she had returned to Egypt. It was scorching hot, even at night. Most were inside their homes but in the centre of the town was an altar to old gods. The altar was partially ruined, and Discordia entertained ideas of obliterating it fully when a figure quietly walked up to it and fell to his knees.

"Please. Pharaoh does nothing. You gods smite us. Why?" His eyes were full of tears and she could see under his clothes he was very thin. "My wife...my daughter... You have taken them from me. No crops grow, I cannot even work..." With shaking hands he put some cuffs and bangles, all of solid gold, at the foot of the altar. "This is all I have left to offer you. I beseech you." His voice waved with exhaustion. "Relent this chaos...or...or release me from this earth..."

"Such a silly request." Discordia made herself visible as she spoke. "Gods do not help any." She placed her hand on the ruined statue where a cracked and broken Anup stood. "The only one who came close to being helpful is gone."

He lifted his head and stared at her. "...Who...who are you?" He blinked, his eyes the colour of cinnamon. His brow furrowed. "Who are you to speak for the gods? You are no pharaoh!"

"I am a god. I am Discordia." Her wings fanned out before folding behind her again. She stroked the statue's cheek. Oh, how she missed him. "I rule the heavens and I do not listen to mortals."

"...Discordia?" The mortal suddenly snatched

the gold from the altar and pressed them to the ground at her feet. "Please. You are the first to answer my prayers. End my torment. Or ease the world's pain. Please. I beg for your mercy." He was on her knees before her, arms stretched out in front of him, nose to the stone ground.

She stared down at him. "Your pleading reminds me of him." She moved her hand from Anup's statue. "Stand. I will allow your land to become fertile again. Take your gold and go, mortal." She wasn't one for being good but something about the mortal eased her.

He lifted his head, somewhat caught in a state of disbelief. His long, thin fingers curled around the gold and he dragged it back to his chest. He stood. "You are wise and merciful." He bowed. "Thank you, a thousand thanks." He backed up, starting to head back to his home when he paused. "...May I dare to ask one more thing of you?"

"What?" Her back was turned to him.

"My wife and daughter. Are they happy? On the other side…"

"If I knew I would tell you." She placed a hand on the statue again. "If I could see or go into the next life I wouldn't be here, I would be with him."

The man's gaze flicked from her to the chipped and weathered face of the Anup statue. The paint and enamel was faded and so the statue appeared blind, his eyes forever closed, waiting to be painted open again. "Him? Anubis? He was your lover? But, I don't understand. You're Greek. Why is this in no tale or prayer?"

"This was long before humans knew of him as Anubis. Once he was called Anup. We broke the rules. He changed me. But they found out and he was punished." She too, was punished but she had merely endured a scrap with a dog. It was nothing compared to Anup's torment. "He wanted me to end him...I did. That is the story. My stories are not happy ones. Chaos thrives because of me. I only do this for you because this was his beloved land."

The man fell silent, his eyes thoughtful. When he spoke he said, "The gods do seem to get pleasure from taking what we love the most, don't they?" He looked at her. "Forgive me. I forgot my place. I meant no disrespect to you, Oh Great Goddess."

"Nothing to forgive. You are right." She turned to look at him again. "What is your name, mortal?"

"Anen."

"Anen." She said his name softly. "You almost remind me of Anup."

"From you, that is a great honour." His words were quiet. "Will I get to see you again?"

"Perhaps," her voice still held the same soft tone.

Anen took one last look at her then headed to his empty home. As he turned away he saw her press her lips to the statue's cheek.

<><><>

Discordia was true to her word. This small village outside of Alexandria became bountiful, and Anen and his neighbours were able to sustain themselves well through the seasons.

Months passed before Anen stood at the small shrine again. He placed a plate of bread and dates and cherries at the feet of the statue. After the food offerings, he pulled a small wooden carving from his robes. It was in the likeness of Anup, only wood brown instead of black. He stood it by the platter, and knelt.

"Thank you for this bounty, fair and merciful Discordia."

"I'm far from fair and merciful, mortal." Discordia was sitting upon the head of Anup's statue, swaths of scarlet fabric of her dress draped over the statue's eyes. She stared down at him. She was not going to take away what she had given his people, but calling her merciful...that was far from the truth of what she was.

He licked his lip and lifted his head to her. "True, then," he said. "Honest. You say what you mean to do, and you do it." He spread his hands out to the offering. "My humble thanks to you."

"Your thanks is not needed." She flapped her wings, lowering herself to the ground before him. She picked up the wooden figure. "You made this?"

He nodded, and moved to pinch the tiny little

lever sticking out from the figure's back. He pulled it down, and the little wooden god's arm rose and he brandished a small ankh. "If it's not to your liking I will take it back."

"It's amazing," she actually smiled a bit. "You have a talent, Anen. You nearly captured his exact likeness in the figure."

"Thank you," Anen said with great humbleness in his voice. "The plate is also for you."

Discordia could smell the dates, the cherries, the wine. It reminded her of the sweet moments between the healing bath and his soothing touch. It made her wings ache, as old wounds are wont to do. Her wings shook slightly as she gazed down at the plate. The memories were bitter sweet. "Thank you."

He bowed his head and stepped back. "Enjoy your meager gifts," Anen said. Then he retreated, to give the goddess her privacy.

<> <> <>

Discordia soon returned to Olympus, with the juice of fruits on her tongue and the tiny wooden toy cradled in her palm. She settled herself on her throne and studied the figurine. She rolled it around in her fingers and made his little arm rise and fall with a nudge of the lever. She couldn't help but smile. The craftsmanship was beautiful. She felt her heart twinge in sadness. Oh, how she missed him. All she had accomplished felt meaningless in his absence.

She looked up from her idle play when

Avarita the Greedy walked into the throne room.

"Mother! Ira and Gula have destroyed everything. I have nothing and I want *everything* and I have *nothing*. Nothing but ashes."

"Perhaps you could make something, then destroy it. You could make the grandest city and do what you wish with it." She lifted the arm of the crafted doll. "It will be something that is only yours, and not theirs."

Avarita crossed his four arms and looked at his mother with contempt. "I don't want to make something. I *want*..." His voice went silent as he saw the doll. "What is that?" He walked up the dais to the throne.

"A gift," she said simply. "It is the image of your father."

His eyes focused on it, then suddenly his four arms were on her. Discordia's wrists were grabbed and her arms pulled down, another hand on her throat, while the fourth swiped the doll from her palm. Avarita closed his fist around it and there was a chilling crack. He opened his hand to look at the toy but the tiny Anup was now in pieces. His limbs were splintered, his nose severed from his face, his body not even worthy to feed a fire.

Discordia's face was frozen, the expression becoming deadpanned. She snatched the remains from him. "Leave my sight." She snapped at Avarita, furious at her son.

Avarita backed up, then quickly scampered

away on all six limbs. He knew to give his mother her space.

She held the little broken figure in her hands, staring down at it sadly. Her wings fanned out and beat the air. She took off, back down to the little village.

She landed beside the statue again and leaned against the carved Anup while she held the smaller, destroyed version in her hands.

It was long after sunset and hours before sunrise until Anen came to her. He shuffled down the path, a blanket wrapped around him to ward off late night chill. He stopped at the foot of the altar and looked at her. His eyelids were heavy, and shadowed with sleep.

"What are you doing here?" He asked in a dazed voice. Was he dreaming?

"One of my children," she showed him the broken Anup, "He was greedy and wanted to take it. He crushed it."

Anen murmured and held out his hand to take the broken toy. "There are worse things," he said with a shrug. "It's just wood. Another can be made, in time."

"But you worked on it, and it was such a beautiful thing." Discordia was truly upset over such a small thing being ruined.

Anen's shoulders were half-way through a shrug when he noticed the tears balancing dangerously off the cliffs of her eyelashes. He eased his shoulders down as to not offend and spoke.

"Don't weep," he said quietly. "You're far too strong to shed tears over a little toy."

"But so few things remind me of him." Discordia said, looking at Anen.

"I don't believe that's true." Anen said. "Every time you and I speak, you mention him. You were upset and so his statue is the first place you come. You replenish our land for his sake."

"But it still is not him." She touched the arm of the statue.

"Nor will it ever be," Anen said. "He's gone, as are my wife and daughter. I don't know if we'll ever see them again, but it doesn't mean we fall apart. You're a goddess. You're not a scared child. You're destruction. Or has your love for him made you weak?"

"I am far from weak," she growled at him, her wings arched. "Have you forgotten the chaos which reigned around you such a short time ago so easily?"

"No, I haven't." Anen answered with quiet, steady calm. "Have you?"

"No." She moved closer to him, her wings spread. It almost seemed like she intended to harm him, her eyes were narrowed as she stared at him. She grabbed his arms, her grip tight and pulled him close. Her lips pressed against his roughly.

Anen was shocked and he allowed himself to be kissed. It seemed unwise to fight a goddess.

"You remind me so much of him," Discordia

said as she pulled back.

He held her at arm's length. "You're seeing what you want to see, Discordia. Not what is actually there."

"I know." She pulled out of his grip. "And I see what is there. I know you are not him, after all, you are nothing but a filthy mortal."

She watched as Anen's gaze clouded over with ambivalence. He lowered his hands. "Come back in a few days and I may have a new toy for you." His voice was dismissive, almost business-like. He wrapped the blanket around his body then left her where she stood.

She left without a word. She was a swirl of emotions, sadness, need, anger. Her wings flapped as she went back to Olympus, sitting upon her throne. The chaos below reigned fiercer than before. Everywhere surrounding Anen's village suffered terribly. His village, Hardia, was the last truly prosperous place.

<><><>

A day passed, Anen was sound asleep in his bed. Wood shavings were sprinkled along his bedroom floor, and a partially shaped lump of wood was laying on his mattress. A shift of weight and pressure on his hips guided him from unconsciousness. When he opened his eyes, he saw Discordia above him, wings tucked behind her. He blinked.

"I am dreaming again."

"Do you dream of such things often?" Discordia asked. She was curious as to why he said *again*.

"The other night," Anen explained. "When you kissed me. It wasn't a dream?"

"It was not." Discordia ran a finger along his jaw. "You may be a mortal and not him, but I do want you."

His eyes narrowed. "You want me. A filthy mortal? That is was what you called me, wasn't it?"

"I was angry," she stated. Her wings made a curtain around them, making the bedroom even darker. "And I would prefer to have you over some toy."

Anen tried to sit up but Discordia pressed him against the bed.

"I am guessing you have known the same feelings." She looked down at him, keeping him pressed down beneath her.

His irises flickered around the white plain of his eyes as he looked up at her and studied her face in the dark. "And if I try to say no?"

"I would honor that." Her finger traced his jaw line. "I would disappear from here, you would be left as the rest."

Judging from his expression, it was not the answer he had expected to hear. "Not very chaotic of you."

"Oh," Discordia smiled sweetly. Apparently he had not fully understood her meaning. "You will be thrown back to the way I found you. Your village will become a victim of my perfect world as it was before I decided to be merciful. Make your choice."

Anen swallowed. His wife had loved this land. The small bluff overlooking the Nile, where she would often eat her lunches and just watch the light shimmer off the water's surface. His child playing with her friends in the footpaths and walkways. Anen could not let this place fall as had so many other lands. He swallowed and nodded.

"Do as you will, oh fair and ruling goddess." There was no malice or sarcasm in his voice. There was not much of anything, just a stale, accepting drone.

Her finger moved from his face, she was surprisingly gentle as her hands explored along his body. Her lips pressed to his, her wings curtained them again.

He did not kiss back. His lips were like a pillow, soft, but un-moving, inanimate. His nostrils flared as he breathed through his nose, the warm air caressing her cheeks and making her white hair flutter softly. Despite his warmth and breath, it was as unenjoyable as kissing a corpse.

"I suggest you become a better lover," she whispered, her lips beside his ear, her warm breath tickled his skin.

He jerked his head away from her mouth and then turned his head to look at her. "I'll let you use me. But I won't let you kiss me."

She looked coldly down at him. "Enjoy the last night of peace." Then she was gone.

<><><>

As humanity endured the chaos, the Olympians bided their time. They submitted to the tortures the Staligia thrust upon them with moans and writhing, but never lost their strength fully. The will of a god was durable.

The Staligia were not always toying with the Olympians. With increasing frequency they traveled down to mankind to whisper sweet horror into the collective consciousness. It was when they were unwatched that the Olympians schemed.

On this day of days, when Discordia's rage was piqued and focused like a splinter-point on Anen, they executed their plan.

The Staligia were the first to return to Olympus, before their mother, and they were gorged on pain and slaughter and terror, lackadaisical.

They wandered into the throne room in a noisy cluster, some moving faster than others, Ira the fastest of all. Once they realized they were without their mother, like all children, their volume and boldness grew.

Avaritia, who had long forgotten the incident with the toy, bounded towards the thrones. He was nearly atop the dais and about to put a grasping hand on the armrest when he felt a burning fist clamp down around an ankle. He looked over his shoulder and saw Ira a moment before his older brother flung him away from the seat and across the throne room.

Ira enjoyed watching Avaritia sail through the air, and did not notice that Superbia took this moment to settle into the throne herself.

Then all merriment came to a swift and distinct end as familiar chains lashed at them like whips. Each link was imbued with the most powerful lightning which arched from one sibling to the other. For all their bluster, the Staligia were still only children, easy to overcome when surprised.

Ira managed to evade some harm and even gripped the charged chain. He stood in defiance for many moments but it was futile as he collapsed, subdued by the power in the chains coursing through his form. In the end, he could see only white lightning.

Zeus appeared in the throne room, shadowed by the other high Olympians. He took in the scene, basking in the success of his trap. The same chains that, for all these years after the coup, Luxuria used to bind him to his bed, the chains he used to bind Anup in his last days, now completely ensnared these bastard children. He waved his hand, and Athena and Artemis stepped forward to tighten the godling's bonds, then dragged them together to the center of the throne room.

The Grecian gods forced cup after cup of Dionysus' wine into the godlings, flavored with serpent venom to numb their bodies and make them small in their weakness. Now secure in their bondage, small and unconscious, the children were placed by Zeus into a simple earthen clay jar.

Zeus darkened the clouds around Olympus and forced the winds to race and the thunder and lightning to wrestle angrily. The storm would grant them a bit of extra security from Discordia's return.

Despite the storm, the Olympians knew they had to quickly be rid of the jar and as they had planned, Athena and Hephaestus completed their forging of a protector, a sentinel to stand watch over the imprisoned children of chaos.

From the clay of the earth they fashioned a woman, upon which each god bestowed a gift. Beauty, charm, grace, the weaver's skills, voice. Fully formed, her eyes opened to the world. Zeus anointed her with a kiss on her brow and held out the jar. "Pandora," he said, naming the being, and placed the jar in her waiting arms.

As the final part of their scheme Artemis escorted her to the home of the titan Epimetheus. They presented her to him as a gift and a wife. Here, away from Olympus she would be safe from Discordia's influence, and the godlings secure in their prison.

At the sight of the darkened clouds, Discordia knew something was amiss. Her rage towards Anen was forgotten quickly. The storm winds proved to be a bother as they tried to wrestle her away from the mountain. Though she eventually managed to navigate the storm, the effort to do so only angered her further.

As she landed beside her throne she took in the scene. Everything appeared as she had left it, her brother still cowering at the foot of the dais. Then she sensed it - an emptiness in her perception her children normally took up. She let out a hate-filled scream as the feeling of loss and loneliness filled her essence. Her children were gone. The only thing she had left of Anup.

She had no grace, only rage as she stalked off the dais and struck her bound brother's side with her foot.

"Where are they?" she screamed. "Tell me where they are!"

Ares only laughed at her, a strong, boisterous, cutting laugh that seemed too powerful for his weakened state. She had been gone too long and Ares had, it appeared, regained some of his warmongering strength. She kicked him again, then grabbed him by the hair and gripped the soft front of his throat. She could feel the inside twitch and vibrate as he continued his booming laughter.

She scowled, sneered, her face a frightening visage of fury. Then Discordia realized that she should be feeling the metal of his toothed collar, not his hot, slick, rumbling flesh.

Ares' fist came at her like a mace and cracked

her on the skull. She fell and skid along the marble floor but quickly got to her feet with a snap of her wings.

Ares was free.

"Who freed you from your chains?" Discordia demanded. "Where are my children?" She glanced to where Seth's cage was displayed and saw that the diminutive chaos god was still inside. So, whoever freed Ares did not bother with the Egyptian. Her gaze returned to Ares and her wings fanned out in warning.

"I will not ask you again."

A burning agony filled each part of her as once more lightning coursed through her entire body. She was so focused on Ares she did not see Zeus nor his wife appear. When the lightning relented she was nearly on her knees, having only the throne to keep her balance.

"You."

Through hazy sight Discordia saw Hera. She wore a veil that hid her face and front, and all that was bare were her arms, upon which her flesh was a tragic disaster of burns and scars. Discordia could not help but smile at the gruesome sight.

"You took from me my beauty. My husband. My throne. My title. All I cared about, all I loved. Now, with your children disposed of, you know my pain. *Our* pain. Do you still find your chaos sweet?"

Her rage became greater, and from it she tore power, power which seeped forth to infect the mountain itself. The floor began to shake violently as an earthquake hit the kingdom of the gods. She was chaos, and she let them see exactly what that meant as cracks in the pillars that held up the vast ceilings around them grew from nothing, toppling great stones down around them as they danced on the buckling tiled floors. She stood as they continued to watch in dazed amazement as the throne room collapsed around them, her hate radiating with each beat of her wings.

"I will find them!" she screamed, "I will rescue them! And then we will return to empty this pantheon once and for all! And your bones will become ash as this entire mountain burns to the ground with my vengence." She turned quickly as Zeus and Ares both reached for her, stumbling amongst the quake and ruin. With a flash of light and heat that burned their outstretched fingertips, she was gone.

Many mortal months passed in a blur that seemed like days for her as she searched for her children. Discordia worked tirelessly, her rage sustaining the chaos she wrought as her search weaved its way across the world. She focused on the places that she thought the elder gods might choose to hide her precious ones. Cursed lands where titans walked held nothing but despair, lakes alive with magic and beauty contained nothing she wished for, mountains with caves dark and deep... the search was fruitless. She rushed through the oceans and seas but found no sign of them. As she screamed back and forth from the four corners of the Earth, from sea to sea, from every land with its patchwork quilts of grain and corn, she was forced to eat her strength just to fuel her anger. She was becoming a thin, wailing ghost of herself.

But she would willingly shed everything if it helped her find her spawn.

During her search, Anen's humble village was forgotten, and Olympus was forgotten. Zeus regained his throne amongst the rubble with the healing Hera at his side. The Olympians knew that to secure their freedom they needed to find a way to strike against her before she had the chance. The gods knew their next chance to strike would come eventually. They would bide their time and once again grow their strength as the earth suffered Discordia's wrath. They believed in their infallible plan, that her children would never again be found or set free.

Discordia finally caught feeling of her children in a very old mountain in a forgotten range that existed since the world was born. She had heard stories of titans still wandering the earth as Zeus allowed it, and this place, untouched by time seemed to speak the truth to those rumours.

She collapsed to her knees, her wings drooping allowing the beautiful feathers to touch the dirt. Weakened beyond what she thought possible, she snuck into the mountain. The year of searching had drained her reserves and left her gaunt, yet the goal of these weary days was now in sight and with it, renewed strength. As she entered the vast cavern beneath the mountain she spotted a woman in a far corner, plainly dressed and tending to sweeping the makeshift stone room in which she inhabited. It was a simple two walls that met in a corner in the vast hall, with bookshelves, a bed, a fireplace and other trinkets adorning it. A fine place for a human amongst the stalactites, mud and chirping bats residing the cave. A meagre living, an ignorant one.

Pandora's lovely voice echoed off the walls as she hummed a sweet bird-song to herself as she tidied her home.

On a shelf by the fire Discordia found her eyes focusing on a simple earthenware jar. It had no markings, no adornments. Despite this, Discordia felt the jar tug at her and she knew that vessel contained her children. Her search was finally over.

With what little strength she had left from her rage, she knew she could not face the titan. Discordia did not see the titan, perhaps he was hunting for the evening supper. She moved in shadows, powling behind vast stalagmites and inching towards the woman. While cautiously stalking Pandora, Discordia began formulating a plan to get the jar without arousing the attention of the titan. For all she knew, he could be looming, or return at any moment. Discordia paused near enough to the woman to hear her catch her breath between the notes of her tuneless song, and Discordia had her idea. Curiosity would be her chaos, the instrument to free her precious children.

Pandora hummed a more chaotic tune as she swept, and soon found herself by the hearth. She felt the warmth of the fire creep up her side and she smiled, imagining she could see the warm gust of air as it rose from the flames. As her gaze followed the imaginary sight her eyes rested on the simple clay jar that had sat on the hearth since she arrived in this grand place. Her memory of it was fuzzy, but she remembered quite clearly the titan imposing his will on her, telling her that she should never touch it, never open it. A queer feeling tickled the back of her mind and a flutter thrilled her belly. What could be in there? Something so plain couldn't be so interesting on the inside. She slowly reached out a hand and brushed the jar with her fingers, feeling the unpolished earthenware texture.

As Pandora's fingers traced up the jar, the feeling inside increased. She wondered what could be so important to keep hidden? Perhaps precious jewels? She could almost imagine the lovely sparkle. Or maybe there was something even more beautiful than jewels? Pandora bit her lower lip and carefully lifted the jar from the mantle with both hands, and brought it to her bosom.

Discordia could hear her children, feel their presence. She watched Pandora cradle the jar as one would an infant. She doted over it, mothered it. It made Discordia sick.

Pandora looked around, suddenly nervous the titan may see her. Still cradling the jar she tip-toed into the darkness away from her fire, behind an ancient rock formation. Now under the cover of darkness Discordia came up behind the girl. She touched Pandora softly, her body immaterial to Pandora's eyes. Her hands glided along the girls side, resting on her slender hips. Discordia's fingers curled around Pandora's hip and slid up, tumbling over the girl's ribs. She leaned her head into Pandora's ear.

"What sights to behold..." Her whisper was seductive. Her hands traced Pandora's stomach and pressed, low, well under her navel.

Pandora's grip on the jar loosened. "Show me these sights..." Pandora whispered as her curiosity grew stronger.

Discordia nipped the lobe of Pandora's ear, her breasts pressed to the young girl's back. The weight Pandora couldn't see made her lungs feel heavy with anticipation. Discordia raised her hand and her fingers scratched at the back of Pandora's scalp, the curiosity pricking her mind.

The lack of any visible source of these urges made it all the more exciting for Pandora. The touches made her skin tingle, wondering what it was, wondering what it would show her. Wondering. She felt fingers glide down, tracing her breasts. It sent sparks of excitement through her.

Discordia lifted her hand to join Pandora's

where it rested on her breast. Their fingers curled together and Discordia placed Pandora's hand on the lid of the jar. Her hand covered the lid and after a swift tug, it was opened and Pandora peeked inside.

Superbia the Prideful was the first to burst from the jar, followed by Ira who moved nearly as swift and twice as messy as the spray from a slit throat. The others spilled forth like sludge and bile, blood and rocks, tumbling violently over one another in a shower of broken chain links, all hurried to feed their starved bloodlust. All except for Tristitia the Hopeless, who was far too morose and who had all but grown into the clay and had become part of the jar wall.

Pandora gasped and hurriedly shut the jar lid. She hugged the jar to her chest and looked around, praying her guardian did not see her sin.

The newly free Staligia paid no mind to Pandora or the titan that was now lumbering through the cavern towards the scene. Nor even to their mother, who raised her hands and laughed in triumph. They loosed themselves upon the lands.

Including that one untouched region in Egypt.

It was then Discordia remembered.

"Anen..." and then she was off, flying towards him. Until now, she had forgotten her anger. Even if she hadn't, if anyone was going to lash out upon him, it was going to be her. But in this moment she did not care. She had wanted to make his land the last good one so long ago. He had shown her kindness despite her cruel moments.

Discordia snapped her wings to get another burst of speed, but then every muscle in her body clenched with an electric fire and she plummeted through the air. Memories flooded her mind, of being ripped away from Anup's heated embrace and tumbling along the sands.

Lightning, she had been once again struck by lightning.

She cursed, catching back up to her pace after fighting herself. Her muscles screaming in protest as her wings beat the air. The village was in her sights. She didn't bother going to the statue, she needed to find Anen, though she knew there was nothing she could truly do to save him.

Discordia flew, weaving through the air to avoid Zeus' bolts. The moon was high in the sky now, a perfect smile in a sea of black and stars. Discordia was so focused she did not see Artemis perched within its curved shape like a seat, nor that Artemis had drawn her hunter's bow.

Artemis loosed three arrows, each finding its mark sweetly, piercing Discordia's wings and the centre of her spine.

Discordia fell to Earth, just beyond the welcoming gates of his city.

"We have given you so many chances, Discordia." Zeus' voice sounded noble, yet booming. He pressed his sandaled foot to her back. "And yet you defy us. No more. Your terror comes to an end on this night."

Discordia screamed in anger, she grabbed an arrow from her wing, the arrow had ruined the beauty of her dark feathers. She stabbed the point into the side of Zeus' foot.

Zeus howled in pain, but then grabbed her hair, wrenching her to face him. He lifted her off the ground, ignoring her pesky kicking and scratching.

"ENOUGH." His meaty fist closed around her throat. "You have wrought countless depravities upon mankind. You and your unnatural bastard spawn. I want nothing more than to make you suffer as you had made us suffer. Your son disfigured my beautiful wife, your daughter drained me of my potent seed!"

"It'll be nice to have less of your filthy spawn crawling around in the mortal world," Discordia sneered. "All should bow down to my daughter for ridding you of your seed!"

"To say nothing of your own bastards and their destruction. Perhaps it is the best place for you. On Earth, to experience the chaos first-hand, all the suffering, stripped of the ability to control it. Have you ever before felt vulnerable, Discordia?"

"I will never feel vulnerable, no matter what you do!" She struggled in his grip. In a show of defiance, her wings gave a number of weak flaps.

"All mortals are vulnerable," Zeus said simply, the air around them going dead and silent. He placed a hand on her wings and arcs of lightning surged through them until the soft pinions caught flame. Her wings burned away, swirling to ash in the wind. The heat from the cleansing fire charred her horns until they cracked and dashed into soot which fell into her white hair like dirty snowflakes.

"You bastard," she snarled, glaring at him over her shoulder. "Taking those away will not make me mortal, fo--"

Zeus did not let her finish her comment or her childish name-calling. His free hand crackled with all the power of the heavens and he thrust his knuckles against her back. Blazing forks of white-hot pain stabbed at her heart, again and again as the lightning forced its way through every part of her core, her being. Her heart stopped and everything was black.

When Discordia awoke, Zeus was gone. She felt so weak. She shakily stood and looked around. These few acres of good land were like an oasis in the middle of nothingness. She took a moment to order her thoughts. But even at night, the sweltering African heat was stifling. The inconvenience of heat was something to which she was not accustomed. She only knew its warmth, its pain, its power of destruction, but not the nagging aggravation of it, the slow torture, the passive aggression. Then she saw the weathered stone Anup standing alert, the stone a cool grey, his face looking deeper into the cluster of modest homes. She remembered and began heading towards the village.

Discordia stumbled through the streets. At least she had a goal, something to cling to. She passed an alley, oblivious to the men who huddled in its darkness. Hands grabbed her, around her wrist, pressed over her mouth, and she was thrown down to the ground. They pressed their weight to her. Her back muscles spasmed as she tried to beat them away with her wings, but those had been taken.

Discordia's hands grew free with her struggle and her fists beat against the man on top of her back. She screamed in anger but there was fear laced in her voice. She felt helpless without her powers, weak. The world spun as she was flipped onto her back. They pried her legs apart while her fingers raked through the sand as she scrabbled for escape. The man above was a smelly, hairy old sleaze with a scar forcing an eye closed. In a strange moment of detachment, Discordia found that he resembled Zeus, only far more unkempt. He swung his fist across her face with such force her neck popped and sparks obscured her vision.

The other one held her legs open, but she managed to jerk her leg and it connected with his groin. He began to fall away and she brought her heel down on his tender lap once more. Her searching hand curled around something awkwardly shaped, with a sharp edge and a blunt side. A rock.

She smashed the rock against the side of the smelly old man's head, the rough, sharp side connected with his skull. Blood seeped out of the gash she left and dripped onto the sands.

Discordia crawled to the man and bashed the rock against his head a few more times for good measure. She was crying, and a burning chill was running through her body at such speed it made her vibrate. Fear. This was fear?

The other man moaned and she whirled, falling on her behind in the sand. She forgot about him. She pounced and the rock connected with his nose. When she lifted the rock, she saw the blow left a crater in the centre of his face. She bashed again, this time she left the rock there.

Discordia shook, breathing heavily. She had to use the wall of the alley to support her shaking legs. Tears slipped down her dirty cheeks and left little trails. Warpaint in reverse.

The walk to Anen's home had become a much longer one than she expected, her body weaker than when she first started the journey. She panted softly as she leaned against the doorframe. His door frame. Her fist shook as she tapped her knuckles on the door.

Many seconds, as well as a few more feeble knocks, passed before Anen opened the door, and Discordia, newborn, brutalized, human, fell into his arms.

Anen fumbled but managed to catch her,

somewhat. He lowered her to the ground. "Miss?" No hint of recognition was in his eyes, on his face. "Miss?"

"You don't remember me..." Discordia sighed, looking up at him through half closed eyes before she let her exhaustion take over.

Water was dripping, too fast to be a leak, too close to be rain. She felt a cool wet cloth on her brow. Water drops slipped down her temples and rolled into her dirty hair. Her lids opened slowly, her icy blue eyes looked around, then she focused on the man pressing the damp cloth to her skin. She reached out, she wanted to be sure it was not a dream. Her arm shook with the effort.

Anen looked down at her while gently patting her brow with the cloth. "I think you suffered a bit of heat stroke," he said. "Here, drink this." He brought a cup to her lips and tipped it lightly so she could taste the tepid, slightly cool water.

She drank, she had never before been so thirsty. Her lips were chapped and peeling from the heat and lack of water.

"Thank you," she said as he pulled the cup from her lips.

"What are you doing out here in the middle of the night?" Anen asked as he set the cup aside. He refreshed the cloth from a bowl of water and wrung it out before placing it back on her brow to cool her skin.

"I came to warn…" She muttered softly, her eyes rolling from left to right in apparent delirium. "There's something going to come. Something other than the chaos that is everywhere. It will not spare any of the villages…" If he didn't recognize, then she wouldn't bring up who she truly was. It may be easier this way, she didn't have the strength to convince him of such minutiae.

He brought the cup to her lips again. "It seems I've found myself a soothsayer." He sounded amused. "I know it's coming. There's no reason why it wouldn't. I've prayed and prayed and gave all I have to the gods, but they refuse me."

"It is the Greek gods in control once more. The others have fallen." Truly, she had simply forgotten about him until she realized what her children were going to do. "You should find somewhere safer to go."

"There is no where to go." Anen said with a tone resigned to defeat. "Everything is fire. It all burns. The Nile is red with blood." But he didn't sound discouraged. "Even if I could go, even if I had a safe place, I am not sure I would want to leave." His face fell. "My wife and child are buried here. They died here. If I am to die anyway, it seems wrong to leave them."

"At least you have something waiting for you there," she sounded bitter.

He lowered his head. "If what you say about

the Greek gods is true...then maybe I don't."

"No one does. Not anymore." She looked away from him. She felt helpless.

They sat in silence until Anen stood from his stool and went to a carafe on a table. He poured out two small cups of wine before he returned. He handed her a cup and helped her to sit up.

"To no more?" He suggested as he raised his small cup.

She couldn't help but smile, just a bit. "To no more." She raised the cup slightly, her arms still weak.

Anen touched his cup to hers and drank. From over the rim of his cup, his eyes watched her. Discordia was sad, it was obvious in her expression and movement. She drank the wine, closing her icy eyes. She looked so fragile, almost like a doll.

"Another?" He offered after downing his wine. Both of them were acutely aware the wind outside was starting to moan and dusting the walls of the town with sand.

Discordia gulped the rest of the wine. She sighed, "Wine is a rarity for me."

"Might as well enjoy the little pleasures while we can." Anen stood from the stool and grabbed the wine. He brought it back to the seat and filled their cups. Another touching of glasses and he drained his wine.

She did the same and felt the wine warm her. She poured another cup, and another.

The winds kept howling and all the pair did

was make small talk which grew more and more slurred and stilted and fettered with giggles inspired by nothing. Then, Anen began to regale her with a tale.

"This...chaos...this...end of times. She was so...mysterious. And, heh, delusional. And lovesick. But...so sad. Kind of how you look right now." He looked into his cup. "She loved him, she said. And I believe her. Believed?" He raised his heavy head to look at her. "Oh, I really angered her." He lifted his hand and spread his fingers over his shaved skull. "She was going to bring all her wrath upon me!" He laughed, loud, leaning back so his chest was puffed out. "All her wrath! The wrath of a lover scorned!" His laughter rose, and then broke apart, becoming heavy thuds of sound, then silence. "But she never did…" He slouched in his stool. "Don't know why." He looked at her with drooping red eyes. "Not worth it, I suppose. I'm just one man."

Anen half-smiled sadly at her, and closed his eyes. His body went limp like an abandoned doll, and the sound of his soft, gentle snores floated to her ears.

She looked away after his little tale. She was unsure whether she should try to tell him. Probably not the best idea, even in her drunken state she knew that well enough. She felt the need to move around and scooted out of the bed. She stretched, her bones cracked which made her flinch. Never had she heard her body make such noises. She looked at the sleeping Anen, her hand was unsteady as she touched his cheek. Her hand dropped heavily to her side and she began to wander around the home, curious about it more than she had been as a goddess, but only marginally.

She opened the wood shutters and looked out the window. They were coming. She could hear her children, her boys and girls, laughing and playing somewhere among the swirling storm winds. She could hear them draw out the tormented screams and cries of mankind, using them as puppets and dolls. They would be here for her soon. Her children. It was probably the way it was meant to be.

She let a few tears fall down. Her children would not even realize who she was, they wouldn't take the time to…

She looked away from the window, turning her gaze back to Anen. She sighed and chose to let him rest longer. Perhaps he should die in his sleep. Such a thing would be merciful.

She headed for the door, where she passed his little work table. It was covered in curls of wood shavings, and chips of wood too big to be called splinters. There, in the garden of thin wood sheddings, stood a half-completed Anup. She swallowed and her fingers lightly traced the rough wooden muzzle. Next to him stood a small wooden figurine with fanned feathered wings and a pair of antlers upon the head. The horns were carved from what seemed to be the tooth of some animal.

Her fingers ran over the horns of the familiar looking figure. She spotted something glistening beside it.

A feather. Her feather. She picked it up and twirled the long, black glossy plume.

Keep that even when you pass...

A souvenir...

...wherever you go.

She looked back at the sleeping Anen. The ground trembled under her feet and the walls rattled. Their children would be here soon.

She took the feather and walked to Anen. She moved slowly as to not disturb him too suddenly. She straddled his lap. The feather tickled the side of his face as she gently dragged it along his cheek. When his eyes flickered open, her chapped lips pressed against his. She ended the kiss with a sad smile. "The time is coming. Nothing awaits us beyond. We should enjoy what we can of life..."

Anen blinked up at her, his eyes glassy and red from the wine. He nodded and answered her kiss with his own. He put his hands just above her waist, and pressed her against his lap. He seemed eager. Perhaps he hadn't taken a lover since his wife.

Discordia's tongue slipped past his lips, they both tasted like wine. She wore nothing but a loose, draped dress, which seemed designed to fall off her body easily. His hands went under the gathered folds of her dress and it dropped off and pooled around her. He looked at her full nude body and his teeth took a breast.

Her hands went to the back of his head, the little prickle of his shaved scalp tickled her palms. She pressed him against her chest more, and her breasts squished against his face. He leaned forward, she leaned back, and the stool threw them both away. Discordia landed hard on the packed floor with Anen on top of her. He fumbled and pulled his robe up over his head and off. He threw it aside where it hit their cups and sent them rolling along the ground.

Discordia lost her breath when they landed and when it returned she gasped. She nipped his ear as his mouth attacked her breasts, his full lips rolling her nipple, his warm tongue dancing around the pale pink bud.

His dick was semi-hard and it brushed against her thigh. He raised a hand and ran it over her dirty, tangled hair. Discordia found the gesture strangely comforting.

One of her legs went around his hips, leaving herself open and waiting, eager for the moment he was ready to take her. She was already wet with need for him. Her hand slipped down his chest and she gripped his slightly hard length in her hand. His body responded immediately to her touch. He sucked on her breasts as if she were a wineskin to be drained and her back arched off the floor. His hips moved forward and she gave him a demanding tug. Both her legs now wound around his hips, and she lead him inside. She moaned as he sucked on her breast, her other hand pressed against the back of his head.

He pushed in with a force she only barely expected. Her human body, though not pure, was subject to things like pain, and needed to adjust for his girth. This was unlike being with Anup, it was clumsy, graceless, yet still so satisfying. She bit her lip.

He rose above her on all fours, with his head still pressed to her chest. Her rear left the ground and he started to move. Sounds of delight fluttered from her throat as the discomfort faded with each wanting thrust. She clung to him, her lips pressing to the top of his head.

His air was restricted by her skin as her breasts pushed to his face, but he liked it. It gave a sort of dizzying sensation, mind-buzzing. Or maybe that was the wine. His hips were strong and he touched deep inside her.

The carnal dance of man was not much different than that of gods, but Discordia found mortal sex to be heavier, messier, prone to moments of unbelievable pleasure, then doldrum awkwardness. At times she would feel the shape of Anen's head, smell his sweat on her skin, hear his moans and be keenly aware he was but a man. Or she would hear a specific inflection in his voice, or the way his hand ran down her body and would recall her lover, her love. Despite how awkward mortal sex could be, she enjoyed it. She ran her hands along his body, the way his body was shaped made her think of *him*.

Discordia yelled with passion and she felt like it echoed in the room. But it wasn't her voice, it was the voices of the townsfolk as the horrors approached. Her spawn were sauntering through the streets like lazy, sluggish water, destroying whatever they fancied. They would reach this humble hut soon. She held Anen tighter and pressed her face to his shoulder.

"Don't stop." She wanted him until the very end. Her children would have to pull them apart themselves. The feather was still clutched in her hand, and she extended her arm, tracing the feather up his spine. Anen shuddered in pleasure at the light tickle. He kissed her, nipping her lip, his tongue sliding against her own. He gave a surprisingly strong buck and broke the wet kiss. He filled her. She tightened her hold around him, she would not let him pull away from her. She kissed the side if his head.

Anen was trembling above her, inside her, and his trembles seemed to seep into the earth and make the hut shiver and sway. But it was her children, she knew.

Outside the blazes that burned only made the night feel even hotter, but the smell of searing meat was mouth-watering to her. She had never known that mankind smelled so nice when roasted. Underneath it all, she thought she smelled a hint of apples.

Anen lifted his head, finally aware of the

chaos happening outside his door.

Discordia grabbed his head in her hands and directed his focus back to her. "Look at me. I said do not stop." She kissed him again, soft this time. Tears slipped from his eyes and ran over her fingers. Her hand left his face and she ran the feather down his chest, his stomach, then back up.

Anen swallowed when the kiss broke. "I do not even know your name," he said quietly.

She ran the feather down between his eyes, over the bridge of his nose, vertically over his lips. There, it came to a momentary rest. She leaned close, her mouth just brushing his as the feather stood like a guard between them. "You do."

Anen's hand covered her's before taking the feather away. He started to speak, but as he did a mist entered into the room. Discordia's gaze left him and Anen's words went unheard. Instead, she heard a sistrum. She looked towards the door, and saw her son. The only one to realize her true identity and he was here to save them from the pain.

His ragged black wings fanned out with a grace and sense of purpose which Discordia recognized from her godly self. The wings closed around them like a shield as the walls came down. She turned her head and looked into Anen's eyes. The dark cloak opened and wrapped around them, enveloping them into the oblivion hidden within.

THE END

ABOUT THE AUTHORS

LILITH K. DUAT is a female in possession of the male gaze and a filthy mind. She has recently found her love for erotica and relishes in reading the hottest she can find and writing out her fantasies. She has a tendency to drag others along for the ride.

MARIA DELYNN wants to experience the fantasies she could never achieve in life, which warped her mind to produce the sexiest writing she possibly can.

Find out more at http://brokenwingsmedia.com

Acknowledgements

The authors would like to thank (in no particular order) the following people for all their help in making this little tale that you are now holding in your hands a reality.

Thank you to J. Lee Kage, Ratslag, Rebecca, Kips, Caelyx, Josh, CM Lovage, Kyle, Dawn, Frankie, Teonova and anyone else who we may have missed.

You know what you did.